Holiday of
the Undead

My Life Among the Undead:

Book 5

Camara M. Bragdon

For more information, or to book an event, contact :
www.camarambragdonauthor.com

Book design by Camara M. Bragdon
Cover design by Camara M. Bragdon

ISBN - 978-1-964265-04-9

My Life Among the Undead
book series

Friend of the Undead

Yard Sale of the Undead

Secrets of the Undead

Carnival of the Undead

DEDICATION

This book is dedicated to my two nieces, Isabelle Tan, and Elisabeth Shorey, who helped create the villainous doll.

CONTENTS

Chapter One:

I Win a Snowball Fight

Christmas is a magical time of year especially in a place like Zephyr where magic is everywhere you look. Those of us who despise winter and all of its cold, harsh realities tolerate the snowy season here. It snows only during December. The temperature never drops below twenty degrees. January and February temps never go below thirty.

Unfortunately, magic wasn't going to help me at the present moment. I had found myself staring through the front door windows at my keys on the kitchen table. For the third time this week, I had locked myself out of my house. I stomped around in my black boots in last night's snowfall to keep the blood circulating in my toes. I jiggled the doorknob for the billionth time, thinking it would open up by using my psychic powers. Sure, I have psychic powers but not the ability to open up locks with my mind.

Let me explain things. My name's Shelly Anderson. My family is from another dimension, another world; call it what you want. When humans come to this magical world, they acquire one magical ability. I'm just your ordinary telepathic librarian who was stranded outside her locked house.

"Super," I said to myself. "It's almost eight-thirty at night, and the temperature's dropping." I wrapped my arms around myself to keep warm. I had been standing outside for almost thirty minutes, and I was freezing my butt off. Hypothermia and I have never been on friendly terms. My roommate, Lisa Miller, was probably at her downtown studio working late again. According to Lisa, being a wedding planner isn't an easy job and is incredibly time-consuming.

I walked around the house for the fourth time, hoping I had missed spotting an unlocked window. After trying all the windows with no success, I headed back towards the front of the house. I took one step and went WHOOSH as my non-treaded boots hit a patch of ice. Seconds later I lay on my back in the cold, wet snow. My purse and its contents were scattered all around me. "I hate winter."

I pushed myself off the ground. My hands might as well have been bare with the flimsy navy blue gloves I was wearing. The tag on them read: "Will keep your fingers warm and toasty." Yeah right! The company's idea of cold was fifty degrees. It was time for drastic measures. I retrieved my cell phone from the snow and hit the speed dial for my boyfriend's phone number.

Eddie Van Helsing picked up on the third ring. "Yo!"

"Why are you answering your phone like that?" I asked him as I put the rest of my purse back together.

"'Cause I felt like it. What's up, Shell?"

"Are you busy right now?" I walked around in a circle to keep warm.

"I just started dinner."

"Good. Could you unlock my house for me?"

"Again? This is the third time this week. I thought you were going to get a spare key."

"If I had, we wouldn't be having this conversation, now,

would we? Please, can you unlock my door? It is freezing out here."

He sighed. "Okay, I'll be right over."

I hung up and trotted into the little shed where my brown-winged horse, Jordan, was sleeping soundly in her stall. The only thing keeping her warm was her soft coat. I shivered as a cold wind swept under the crack at the bottom of the door.

I walked back outside and was hit in the shoulder with a snowball. "What the?" I brushed the snow off my coat as I looked around for the culprit. My boyfriend's sleek carrot-shaped car was parked alongside the road. I was surprised he had brought this car. Whenever it is snowing, he normally drives his picklemobile, a ridiculous, rust bucket in the shape of a pickle. The car is so top-heavy it can't possibly spin out on the ice.

But that didn't bother me at the moment. I had to find the snowball culprit. I packed a snowball the size of a softball and began to hunt down my quarry. The streetlight gave away his position. I spotted him darting behind the car, and I launched my snowball at him. The snow splattered across the hood.

Another snowball came out of nowhere and nailed me in

the chest. This meant war! A green mist appeared and slid under the car. "No fair!" I shouted as I bent down to get more arsenal. "You can't turn into mist!"

"Who says I can't!" the mist shouted back.

His answer gave away his hiding place which was on the left side of my house. I began running as fast as I could towards the mist. "Gotcha!" I said as I tackled him.

The mist quickly transformed into a man in his mid-twenties with curly jet-black hair. I couldn't see his dashing green eyes because he was face down in the snow. The jean jacket I had given him last Christmas was now wet with slush. "Mind removing your knee from my kidney?" a muffled voice asked.

"Sorry," I said as I got off of him.

Eddie scrambled to his feet and brushed the remaining snow off his wet khaki pants. "Nice tackle there, babe!" he said as he shot me a fanged grin. Yep, you guessed it. My boyfriend is a bona-fide, very sexy vampire.

I smiled back at his compliment. "That's why you don't start a snowball fight with someone who grew up around snow."

"Sorry about the snowballs. I couldn't resist!" he admitted. He leaned forward and gave me a quick kiss on the lips. "Does this make you warm?"

In more ways than one, I thought to myself. I wrapped my arms around him. "Somewhat, but my butt's still freezing. Can you hurry up and unlock my door?"

He smiled and wrapped his arms around me as we walked to my front door. He let go of me, changed himself into the green mist, and slid under the door. Once he was inside, he flicked on the kitchen lights. Instead of unlocking the door, he walked over to my kitchen table and picked up my keys. Tauntingly, he dangled them in front of me for a second or two before finally unlocking the door.

"Thank you so much," I said as I sprinted inside, embracing the warmth of my home's furnace.

Eddie tossed my keys to me which I promptly dropped on the linoleum floor. He went to the fridge in search of something to drink. My boyfriend has a severe blood allergy and can't drink blood without puking all over the place. Normally he fulfills his need for blood with fruit and vegetables. But not tonight. "Can I have a root beer?"

"Sure, help yourself," I replied as I went to the bedroom to change out of my snow-soaked clothes. Closing the door behind me, I peeled out of my navy blue pants and pink and white long-sleeved tee and threw on a pair of clean jeans and a purple sweatshirt with flowers on it. "Cricket had her baby," I said through the door.

The pop of a soda tab could be heard before he answered. "What did she have?"

"A girl," I replied as I ran a comb through my brown hair and then threw it up into a wet ponytail. "I told her we would visit her tomorrow." I came out of my bedroom in dry clothes.

Eddie was leaning against the kitchen counter sipping his root beer. "You do realize we are going to that movie tomorrow night?"

I nodded. "Yeah, we can go to the later showing and grab some fast food on the way."

"Sure, that's no problem." After tossing the empty can into the recycling bin, he kissed me before heading out the door.

"Hey," I said, "what happened to the picklemobile? I

thought it drives better in the snow than all your other cars.”

“The muffler fell off.”

“Completely?”

“Yep! Spent a good chunk of my day off yesterday replacing it.”

“You should get rid of that thing,” I told him as I took the empty teakettle off the stove. I turned on the kitchen faucet and filled the kettle with water. Even though I was in dry clothes in a nice, warm house, I was still chilled. Plus, I had an intense craving for a cup of French vanilla cappuccino. “Want some?” I asked.

Eddie shook his head. “No thanks, babe. I really need to leave.” Then he continued our conversation. “I can’t get rid of the picklemobile. You’d miss it too much!”

I rolled my eyes at him. “Why have you held onto it for so long?”

“I won my first race with that car.”

My telepathy is limited just to the minds of the undead. So when Eddie mentioned this particular race, he was thinking about the six-inch-high, gold-painted plastic trophy that was sitting on the bottom shelf of the display case in his garage. "Fifth place," I reminded him as I put a couple of scoops of the drink mix into a coffee cup. "You didn't get a trophy, you got a participation award."

Eddie knew I was having trouble imagining the picklemobile speeding down a racetrack. "Well, back then, the car didn't shake violently when it reached sixty miles per hour. It could go some pretty sweet speeds. One time, I clocked it going one-twenty. And, it was the first car I built."

"And the first car you have probably spent the equivalent of a mortgage payment on it for repairs."

"But it's still running."

I shook my head. Hell would freeze over before Eddie would sell that car. The teakettle whistled, and I turned off the stove. I glanced down at my watch. "You'd better get back to work."

"Yeah," he replied, glancing down at his watch, "wouldn't want your dad firing me." Aside from building and repairing cars, Eddie is the night manager at my father's diner. We kissed again, and he started out the door. "I'll pick you up at six-thirty, and don't forget your keys," he called over his shoulder.

I did another eye roll. Pity he had his back turned. It was a good one. "Very funny!"

Chapter Two:
Meeting My Friend's Bundle of Joy

The very next night, Eddie and I arrived at the Zephyr

Memorial Hospital to see my good friend and coworker, Cricket

Lunesta, and her new baby girl. The hospital was a huge,

five-story tan brick building right near the waterfront of the

Sapphire Sea. Eddie parked the carrot car into a parking space

closest to the hospital's main entrance. We got out and sprinted

to the revolving double doors to avoid the bitterly cold wind that

was coming directly from the sea.

The lobby of the hospital was fairly busy with doctors and

nurses rushing back and forth. Several patients were sitting in

the three rows of puke green leather chairs you see in waiting

rooms.

An elfin nurse in her mid-fifties was sitting at the gray

desk. She barely noticed us as she talked on the phone to a patient whom we surmised from the conversation was asking about the best way to get rid of hemorrhoids. Eddie and I exchanged disgusted looks. That sounds painful, I told him telepathically.

I don't even want to think about it.

I nodded in agreement. We waited in silence, trying not to eavesdrop on the nurse's conversation. Finally, she got off the phone. "We're friends of Cricket Lunesta," I said. "She had her baby here yesterday morning. Could you tell us what room she is in?"

Henrietta, that's what her name tag said, gave us a curt nod and began typing on the computer. She looked up from her work. "Mrs. Lunesta is in the maternity ward on floor five in Room 538," she informed us. "Do you know how to get there?"

"The elevators down the hall on your left?" Eddie purposely put his answer in the form of another question.

The nurse nodded and waved us on before answering the phone. As we headed down the white-painted hallway, I looked at my vampire in surprise. "How did you know that?" I asked him.

"Shelly, if you remember correctly, I know this place pretty well."

"Oh, yeah!" I said, realizing to what Eddie was referring. Almost a year ago, I was viciously attacked by gargoyles and was laid up in the hospital for about a month. Of all my family and friends, Eddie was the one who had come the most times to visit me. We started officially dating a month later. "You even came late at night, several hours after visiting hours were over." I reminded him as I pressed the up button on the elevator.

"Your room number was 345. I had to haggle with some pretty tough nurses there. They finally let me see you after I told them the only way you would heal was if you received a daily dose of my love."

I smiled and shook my head at him. "That's so sweet and cheesy, Eddie."

"The nurses bought it, Shelly."

The elevator opened, and we stepped aside to let a couple of doctors and nurses get off. Once we got inside, a mother Welkie with her three kids, one of whom was sitting in a stroller, joined us. Welkies are a race of humans who possess a wide variety of magical powers. The Welkies who practice good magic are known as wizards and enchantresses, but if they perform magic that is harmful or destructive, they are known as sorcerers and witches. The little seven-year-old boy began pressing each one of the floor buttons. He was starting on the path to sorcery early.

"Jonas," his haggard mother told him, "we're only going up to the third floor."

"I like to press the buttons!" the boy retorted.

"But these nice people might not like that," she said.

The four-year-old girl looked up at Eddie and me with innocent eyes. "Why are you at the hospital? Did you bite her? Is she a vampire, too?"

Her mother gave a horrified gasp. "Darcy!" she scolded.

"I'm just asking, Mommy!"

"It's all right," I assured the enchantress. I bent down so I could be at eye level with the girl. "My boyfriend and I are visiting a friend who just had a baby," I told her.

"Mommy had a baby," Darcy commented. "He's really stinky."

"That's because he has diarrhea," Jonas informed us.

I glanced over at Eddie who was struggling not to laugh. He was thoroughly enjoying this conversation with the little kids.

"I'm sure these nice people don't want to hear—," the mother stopped mid-sentence as we all watched the elevator doors open onto Floor Two, and Jonas darted out. His mother gave us a pleading look. "I am so sorry," she apologized.

Because I was the one closest to the door, "Don't worry about it," I told her as I held the door open for her. She hurried off to catch the little fugitive. Eddie shot one of his endearing smiles at me as we waited in the elevator.

"I like snow!" Darcy announced out of the blue after a moment of awkward elevator silence.

"Really?" Eddie asked her. "Do you like snowball fights?" He winked at me, remembering what happened the night before.

The little girl nodded. "Yesterday, Jonas and I had a snowball fight, and then we ate the snow. There are two types of snow: white snow and yellow snow. We're not supposed to eat the yellow snow."

Shall we take bets on what makes the snow yellow? I

asked Eddie subliminally.

I think it would be a tie, Eddie responded.

The enchantress came back with the little rascal in tow. She was scolding him up and down, using all the threats parents usually give to their disobedient children. The rest of the ride up to floor four was silent with the occasional face-making exchange from the two kids. But that was quickly put to rest with the evil eye of their mother. As soon as the family got off, Eddie and I burst out laughing. "From now on, I'll never look at snow the same way again," I said, wiping a few tears from my eyes.

"God, you gotta love kids," Eddie said as we got off on the next floor. The maternity ward was a lot cheerier than the lobby. The walls were painted a bright yellow with pale blue linoleum flooring.

I nodded. I loved the way my vampire interacted with kids. And I told him so. "Someday, you're going to make a really good father, hon."

The vampire gave me a quick kiss on the forehead. "I would like to be the father of your children."

"I would like that," I told him.

"Someday," he replied.

We stopped the conversation the moment we arrived at the large pink receptionist's desk. A vampire nurse was on duty. She was working overtime and couldn't wait to get home to her family. I looked at Eddie. My heart was racing just a bit. He was being truthful about being a father. But not just any father, he wanted to start a family with me. That thought made me smile. I could definitely see that in my future.

"If you could just sign in here, please!" the nurse told us as she handed us a clipboard. Eddie and I scribbled down our names on the check-in sheet, and then we both went to Room 538.

I knocked on the half-opened door and slowly poked my head into the room. "Cricket, it's Shelly," I said quietly so as not to wake the sleeping fairy baby in my friend's arms.

"Oh, come on in, Shelly," Cricket Lunesta said. Fairies in Zephyr are like humans except that they have two large, beautiful moth or butterfly-like wings. At the moment, her light green moth-like wings were gently splayed behind her back on the white hospital bed. Cricket's two feathered antennas rested back against her dark hair. "Come say hello to Rosie," she whispered. "She's just waking up."

Eddie and I walked into the room. I peered at the tiny baby. "Can I hold her?" I asked tentatively.

"Of course," Cricket replied.

I took off my winter coat and asked Eddie to hold it for me. Then I carefully took the newborn in my arms. Rosie opened her purple eyes and looked up at me. "Hey, precious," I said to her. "Look who's got her mother's eyes."

Cricket nodded. "But she's got Max's hair!"

I brushed back the blanket covering Rosie's tiny head to reveal a head full of red hair. "And a whole head of it, too."

Eddie looked over my shoulder at the infant fairy. "She certainly does," he agreed.

"Want to hold her?" Cricket asked him.

"No, thank you," Eddie replied as he shifted the weights of both our coats to the other arm. "I'll let Shelly hold her. She's been looking forward to seeing Rosie all day."

For the next hour, Eddie and I admired the little girl. Cricket looked so radiant with her first child. I kept thinking back to the conversation I had with Eddie earlier. We had talked about marriage and kids before, but Cricket's new baby had made it seem more and more likely. Perhaps the reason marriage was on my mind was because my father was getting remarried in two weeks. I found myself wondering if Eddie's comment meant that someday we would get married.

Around ten o'clock that night, Eddie and I were walking towards his car in the TimeMaxx movie theater parking lot. Tiny snowflakes danced in the brisk air as I pulled my green fleece hat over my cold ears. "Well, that movie sucked!" I said.

Eddie pulled up the collar of his jean jacket and then noticed how cold I was. (I'll admit it. I'm a wimp when it comes to cold.) He pulled me closer to him to keep me warm. "I agree," he told me. "That's the last movie recommendation we get from your brother."

"I think we were the only people who actually sat through the entire movie. What did my brother tell you about this movie?"

"Robin said it was supposed to be a great movie with enough scary scenes to have you huddling next to me the entire time.”

I rolled my eyes. “Well, I think Attack of the Killer Marshmallows should have been a dead giveaway. The acting was horrible. Sesame Street has better actors.”

“How many death stares did we get?”

“Twelve, I think.”

“They were just jealous of our brilliant and witty commentary.”

“I don’t understand why they were so upset. The movie wasn’t exactly Oscar material.”

“I love going to movies with you, especially bad ones.”

Eddie took the car keys out of his jacket pocket and automatically unlocked the door. He opened the car door for me and then got in on the driver’s side.

My khaki pants slid across the icy black leather seat. “Good god, Eddie,” I told him as I rubbed my bare hands together. “Turn on the heat. It’s freezing in here.”

My vampire turned on the car and flicked the heat to the highest setting possible. “Do you have chronic hypothermia or something?” he asked me as he pulled the car out of the parking lot

"No, it's just freezing in here!" I zipped up my coat all the way and jammed my hands into the arms of my jacket. I smiled when I thought about the awful special effects we had just seen. Imagine Marshmallows coming to life. "Can it really happen? Bringing objects to life?"

Eddie shrugged. "It's possible, but it's really old magic. Giving life to an inanimate object is a spell that went out with the dinosaurs.

"You mean no one practices that kind of spell anymore?"

He nodded. "Magic has progressed over the centuries, and one can do a whole lot more damaging spells than bringing objects to life."

"When you were a wizard, did you ever perform that kind of spell?"

He shook his head. "No, we were never taught those kinds of spells. They had already become obsolete by the time I was born."

"Oh, interesting!" I replied. Magic has always interested me, and with Eddie's history, he's a walking encyclopedia of magic. A very hunky walking encyclopedia, I might add. I'm one of the few people who know my boyfriend was a wizard before he became a vampire. It's not the fact he can perform a small handful of spells that bothers him, it's when people start to ask how he was turned. I know what happened, and it was very painful for him.

We finally arrived at my place. The car had just started to heat up. I unbuckled my seat belt and gave Eddie a warm kiss. "I had a great time tonight."

He kissed me back. "Glad you did. Good night, babe!"

"Good night, love," I told him. I grabbed my belongings and got out of the car. After a few moments of digging through my purse, I pulled out my keys and let myself in.

I waved to Eddie who made sure I got in safely. My eyelids were starting to get very heavy. I got into my green pajama pants and an old pink t-shirt and crawled into bed. But I didn't go right to sleep. My mind was filled with images of adorable, little Rosie and scenes of killer Marshmallows. I chuckled to myself. Imagine inanimate objects attacking people!

Chapter Three:

I Get an Offer I Can't Refuse.

After work the next day, I rode my winged horse, Jordan, over to my friend, Creighton Horsefeather's, for dinner. Creighton is a centaur in her mid-twenties who lives with her divorced mom, her divorced sister, and her niece and nephew in a large, one-floor, ranch-style house with green siding and matching yellow trims. You would think this half-human, half-horse race would be living in a barn. They don't, but I have heard Creighton's mom use that phrase whenever the grandkids leave the front door open.

I walked to the front door and rang the doorbell. Hooves could be heard on the hallway carpet from behind the door. The door opened and Creighton greeted me. "Hi, Shelly," she said as she ushered me inside. "Come on in. Supper's almost ready."

Creighton's black hair was pulled back into a long braid which went all the way down her human back and brushed above her black horse's body. The green scrunchie complimented her deep purple polo shirt. "Oh, is that a new shirt?" she asked, referring to my pink and black checkered Tee.

"Yeah, Eddie got it for me a couple of weeks ago," I replied as I absently brushed some lint off my black jeans. I followed the centaur into the huge kitchen.

Creighton's mom, Fran Sleipnir, or Ms. Sleipnir, as she is better known to her second-graders, was standing at the stove stirring and seasoning a big pot of vegetable stew. She greeted me cheerfully. "Hello, Shelly. I'm so glad you could come."

"Thanks for inviting me, Ms. Sleipnir," I told her.

"Well, sit right down," She said as she poured the steaming mixture of carrots, broccoli, green beans, peas, and noodles into a huge serving bowl. "Dinner is just about ready."

I followed Creighton to a six-person table where Creighton's sister, Gretchen, her seven-year-old niece, Annika, and her six-year-old nephew, Benji, were putting on the remaining silverware. There was only one chair at the table, and it was mine. Centaurs don't use chairs, but sit down on the floor during meals. After offering my help, I sat down and pulled the purple cloth napkin over my lap.

The centaurs gathered around the table, and Mrs. Sleipner ladled out vegetable stew for everyone. "So, how are the wedding preparations for your father and Amelia going?" she asked me.

"Good," I replied as I ate a couple of spoonfuls of the delicious stew. "Dad said it's getting down to crunch time."

"Well, everyone's very excited about the wedding," Mrs. Sleipner answered.

"Amelia's going to look so beautiful in her wedding dress," Creighton commented.

"Yeah, her dress is gorgeous. It's an ivory ballroom gown with pearl-like embroidery swirls along the edges." I said. "She got it from Renfield's.com at a great discount price."

"I bet it has lots of buttons," Gretchen replied. "I knew a lady who had a dress with over a hundred buttons on it. She said it took almost twenty minutes to put it on

I nodded. "It has about twenty or so buttons," I answered,

but I was thinking about my dream wedding dress. It would have no buttons, just a zipper up the back. I shook my head in disbelief. When would I get married? I knew the "who" part. Ever since Eddie and I had started dating, I'd been having fantasies of the two of us getting married.

"Are you and Eddie going to get married?" Annika's question brought me back to reality.

"Annika Chiron!" Gretchen scolded.

I blushed a bit. "It would be nice." I shouldn't be thinking about any other wedding other than my dad's right now. I decided to change the subject. "So, what do you guys want for Christmas?" I asked Annika and Benji.

"I want a chemistry set. Can I get a chemistry set, Mom?" Benji asked as he accidentally sprayed some mangled peas across the table.

Gretchen took a long sip of coffee. "Well, I was thinking of giving you a machete and a vial of arsenic, but a chemistry set works, too." I had to wonder what was in the young mother's coffee.

"Really!" Benji exclaimed, seeming surprised that his

mother would even consider giving him something destructive, considering what happened last Christmas.

"How about a nice pair of mittens?" Creighton suggested as a huge smirk spread across her face.

"At least I want something reasonable," Annika said.

"What's that?" I asked.

"Somona, the talking doll!" Annika replied excitedly.

I looked over at Creighton for an explanation.

"It's a new doll," my friend said.

"She repeats everything you say to her, and she says five of her original phases. It's only $35.95." Annika rattled off the television commercial she had committed to memory.

"And it's being sold exclusively at that new toy store in the Moonlight Mall," Creighton answered. The topic of conversation shifted as Gretchen talked about the college classes that she was taking to complete her bachelor's in teaching. Then Mrs. Sleipner told us about the trying parent-teacher conference she had to endure with a troublesome student. Creighton shared the latest details of her most recent date with the hunky centaur, Tanner. I added the tale of the mischievous kids Eddie and I saw the other night.

Creighton showed me to the door a few hours later. We walked over to where my winged horse was waiting. "Thanks for coming over," she told me.

"It was fun," I replied as I zipped up my coat a bit. Over dinner, I started to get a growing headache along with a runny nose.

Creighton wrapped her arms around herself. "Could you do me a favor?" she asked me.

"What?"

"Well, I told Annika I would get her that doll for Christmas. It goes on sale at midnight tomorrow night at the Toy Carnival."

"Okay," I said, afraid of what she wanted me to do.

"My family's leaving for the mountains tomorrow morning. So, I was kind of wondering if you could pick one up for me."

"What!" I almost shouted.

"Come on, Shelly. It's Christmas!"

I narrowed my eyes at the centaur. "Don't give me that 'it's Christmas; therefore I should stand in line until midnight' crap. What if I have something to do?"

"I'd get it myself, but we have to leave tomorrow. Plus, there aren't any malls up in the mountains."

"What about ordering it online?"

"You know how busy things have been with my grandfather being sick." She had grabbed her purse before we left and was looking through it. Finally, she pulled out forty druci (the equivalent of forty American dollars) and handed them to me. "Here, I'm giving you the money for it."

I pocketed the bills. "Fine, I'll get one for you, but you owe me big time, girl."

"All right. Goodbye, Shelly!"

I climbed upon Jordan's back. "Bye, Creighton. Have a good time at your grandparents." We waved goodbye, and Jordan flew me back home. Super, I was going to spend elghl hours tomorrow night standing in line for a talking doll. If I ever have kids, I vowed, I would not stand in line for hours and hours just for a dumb toy. Love has its limits.

Chapter Four:
Why I Hate Standing in Lines

The next morning I wanted to go back to sleep. My throat felt like it was on fire, but I had to go to work. So, I crawled out of bed and got ready for the day. Because it was a nice, winter day, I decided to give Jordan a break and walked the twenty minutes to work in the fresh snow.

I slowly started to realize I was getting a cold. Crap! I thought to myself as I raced into the staff bathroom at the library to blow my nose for the umpteenth time that morning, I can't get sick right before Dad's wedding. I should've taken some cold medicine before I left this morning. I muddled through the rest of my day before I called a taxi to take me to the twenty-four-hour Moonlight Mall.

Even though this mall is one floor, it has about a hundred

and fifty stores. In the shape of a Y, the mall has two food courts,

a few big-name department stores, and several small specialty

shops and businesses. The Toy Carnival is the only interesting

shop located in the part of the mall that includes an optometrist's

office, a hair salon, an odd-smelling health food store, an

overpriced vacuum shop, a cell phone store, and a computer

store.

As I approached the Toy Carnival, I realized I should have

brought a book to read. The line of eager women, both young

and old, extended from the front of the toy store, past the eye

doctor's office and the vacuum shop, and stopped right in front of

the empty wall between the hair salon and the health food store.

I leaned against the light grey wall, turned on my cell, and

checked my messages. Nothing.

For the next hour, I listened in on conversations from

other prospective doll owners, played one game on my cell

phone until I got frustrated, and ate the last piece of gum buried

in my purse. Finally, I realized how hungry and bored I was

getting, but I couldn't lose my place in line. Time to recruit some company. I hit the speed dial on my cell phone. "You bored?" I asked when Eddie picked up.

"Not really. I'm doing the dishes," he replied as I heard him turn on the kitchen faucet.

"The dishes can wait. Come join me for a fun-filled night at the mall."

"What are you doing at the mall that I should be there for?"

"Creighton coerced me into getting a doll for her niece."

"Okay," Eddie answered, sounding unsure of why his presence was needed.

"The doll doesn't go on sale until midnight, and I'm bored and starving." I looked behind me as a frumpy Welkie in her early four-hundreds was suddenly standing behind me. She set her purple and black floral bag on the floor and unfolded a green canvas chair. She sat down and began knitting something with the needles and the mustard yellow yarn that she retrieved from her bag. "I can't lose my place in line, Eddie."

"You're standing in line?"

I rolled my eyes at the comment. "I need someone to talk

to for the next six hours. Plus, I left Jordan at home, and I need a ride home. So, if you aren't doing anything important—."

"All right, I'll be over in a few. Which mall are you at?"

I told him where, hung up, and waited.

My eyes grew wide the moment Eddie came into my line of sight. He was once again wearing his jean jacket over a long-sleeved navy and white polo with a pair of Leviathan blue jeans. I wasn't excited because he had shown up, but because of what he was carrying. In my vampire's hands were two large iced cappuccinos. "Ooh!" I said. "Which one's mine?"

"The mint one," Eddie replied as he handed me the cup with rich mint drizzle on top of a huge pile of whipped cream. He took a sip of his caramel cappuccino.

I took a long, luscious sip of my drink. The iced coffee soothed my sore throat, and it was delish. "You're a saint, Eddie! From now on, I'm going to call you Saint Edgar, the patron saint of cappuccinos."

"Don't!" he said. "You know I hate my full name. I'll be fine with 'Saint Eddie.' " He glanced around at the growing crowd of people surrounding us. "Wow! I can almost smell the desperation coming from these parents and grandparents trying to fulfill their kids' Christmas wishes for an doll."

"But you're here," I pointed out.

"Only because you asked me to come." We sat down on the floor and leaned up against the wall.

"True," I replied as I took another sip of my drink.

"So, tell me about this doll."

"It's Somona, the talking doll." I unzipped my purse and pulled out a folded piece of paper. "I looked it up online while I was at work, and it's pretty creepy looking."

Eddie took one look at the picture of the green-haired doll in a purple and blue polka dot clown outfit and its ghastly painted face and shuddered. "Whoa! That is creepy. I've seen zombies with prettier faces. Put that thing away!"

I folded the paper back in my purse. "I can't believe you, a vampire, are freaked out by a doll!"

Eddie raised an eyebrow at me. "That's not a doll. It's a spawn of Satan."

"Good point." I decided to change the subject. "Guess

how much Satan's spawn is?"

"Ten, fifteen dollars?" he guessed.

"Almost forty dollars!"

"You're kidding me!"

"I wish, but at least Creighton gave me the money."

Eddie put his arm around me and pulled me close. He kissed me on the cheek. "You're a great friend to her, Shell."

"Yeah, but I won't be doing this ever again."

"While we're on the topic," he said, "have you figured out what we're giving your dad and Mrs. Cross for their wedding?"

"No. Do you still have the gift registry list?"

My boyfriend retrieved his wallet from the back pocket of his jeans and grabbed a tiny bundle of folded-up paper. He held it in the palm of his hand and spoke to it. "Maximum five!" The papers magically grew to their normal size, and he gave them to me.

I dug a pen out of my purse and unfolded the papers. As I perused the contents, I found myself kind of disappointed in Dad and Amelia's suggested gifts. "Crockpots. Wedding clocks. Picture frames. Pots and pans."

Eddie looked over my shoulder and pointed to an image on the page. "Hey, what about that espresso machine?"

"Can't buy it. Someone else already got it." I read the rest of the list, finding nothing of interest. "Okay, we need to go a more creative route."

"Why don't you paint something for them?"

I looked at him incredulously. "And what? Tell them it's from both of us? 'Hey, Dad and Amelia, here's a picture I painted while Eddie gave moral support.'"

"Okay, I get it. Bad idea. Let me think." He glanced back at the list, and his eyes landed on a picture of a wedding photo album. An idea came to him. "No one's bought this one yet. It's nice looking."

Suddenly, a better idea came to me. A gift so perfect and personal that it would touch Dad and Amelia. "Ooh, ooh, even better. We make a scrapbook of their lives together, complete with pictures and various memorabilia."

He looked at me as if I had grown a third nostril. "Shelly, a scrapbook? You want me to do a scrapbook?"

"Please, Eddie? This would mean a lot to my dad and

Amelia. Both of them have lost the photo albums of their first spouses. I think it would be nice to put one together for them."

Eddie was about to suggest another alternative when he realized how much I wanted to make an exceptional present for Dad and Amelia. He didn't want to hurt my feelings, and so he agreed to help. "Sounds good. I'll help with whatever you want me to do."

I gave my vampire a great, big hug. "They're going to love it! And once I get enough photos and memorabilia together, we can do it in about two or three nights."

"Make it two nights, and I'll take you out for dinner at Ambrosia again."

I liked that. Ambrosia is a very high-class restaurant that Eddie took me to on our six-month anniversary. The least expensive item on the menu is twenty-five dollars, but the food is so divine! "Deal," I said as we shook hands.

We were silent for a minute or so until Eddie asked an interesting question. "I've been wondering. Did your dad ever date anyone besides Mrs. Cross?"

I shook my head. "After my mom died, Dad focused on

raising Robin and me. At that point, I don't think he was ready to start dating again."

"Probably as kids, you and Robin weren't ready for a new parent."

"My dad loved my mom so much," I said softly. "Did you know they were high school sweethearts?"

"Nope." Eddie doesn't stop me whenever I'm talking about my mom. He knows that I still miss her, even though she died when I was thirteen.

"Dad got Mom a pretty cool engagement ring."

"Really?"

"Yeah! Here let me show it to you." I unzipped one of the inside pockets of my purse and pulled out a faded black jewelry box. "I always keep it in my purse so I won't lose it."

Eddie took the box from me and opened it. Inside, the once sparkling diamond sat firmly on the golden, three-strand braided band. "Wow!" he said, very impressed. "Your dad has good taste." He closed the box and handed it to me.

I nodded as I gave a little cough. I took another long drink. "It's really pretty. Dad gave it to me on my eighteenth birthday." I began to brighten up as I carefully put the box back in its hidey-hole. "I think my mom would be very happy that Dad's getting married again." I gave a hard cough.

My vampire looked at me with concern. "Are you getting a cold?" he asked.

I nodded as I coughed again. "I think I got it when I locked myself out of the house the other night and getting chucked by a snowball didn't help." My stomach gave a loud growl. "I think I may have given you my cold."

Eddie grinned at me. "Don't worry about it, babe! Vampires can't get sick."

"Lucky you! Then how about getting me some food to make me feel better."

Eddie pushed himself to his feet. "Got any special requests?" he asked before he started to walk towards the nearest food court.

"I don't care. I'm just hungry. Surprise me!" I told him as I settled back against the wall.

He waved goodbye to me. "See you in a bit!"

I watched my vampire walk away, his hands stuffed into

the pockets of his jean jacket.

"Are you and your husband getting a doll for your daughter?" the lady behind me asked as she looked up from her knitting.

I turned to face the woman who was wearing a red winter coat over a pink sweatshirt that said, "Grandma's little Angels: Penny, Drew, and Candace" and a pair of black sweatpants that so did not match the bright green sandals she was wearing with her white socks. "Oh, no!" I told her as I felt the heat rush to my face. "We're not married. I'm just getting the doll for a friend of mine."

"When you two have kids, you'll be standing in lines just like this one."

Only on a cold day in Hell, I thought to myself as I nodded in reply. I studied the woman's face for a second or two before I gave up trying to figure out where I had seen her before.

"I'm getting Somona for my favorite granddaughter, Penny."

"How old is she?"

"She's only five, but she reads at a fifth-grade level. She's very smart for her age. I wish her older sister was as smart as her."

I nodded, not agreeing with what she was saying. I looked at the blue and green yarn thing which was in her lap. "What are you making?" I asked to change the subject.

"Candace's Christmas present," the woman said with a frustrated sigh as if she was giving up the crown jewels. "I'm making her a sweater." Then she brightened a bit. "But, I'm making a dress for the new doll I'm getting Penny. Did you hear the store might not have enough dolls?"

I shook my head. "No." Crap.

"Well, I hope that they have enough. I don't care what it takes. Penny's going to get Somona for Christmas!"

Yeah, I thought to myself, and all poor Candace is going to get from Grandma is a crappy knitted sweater. Merry Christmas! I barely listened as the woman rambled on and on about how great this Penny girl was. How she was the best in her class, in her family, and in the grandmother's mind, the best kid in the whole wide world.

I checked my watch. Good god, where was Eddie? My

stomach growled again, and I picked up my drink and finished off the remaining dredges of my cappuccino. I glanced over at the half-empty mint cappuccino. Eddie wouldn't notice if I drank it. The demons of temptations took over my body, and I finished off the drink as I waited for my boyfriend and the food.

"Shelly, what are you doing with my cappuccino?"

I nearly choked on a piece of ice the second I heard my boyfriend's voice. "Nothing!" I replied the second I was able to speak. I quickly set the empty cup back on the floor.

Eddie shook his head at me. He handed me one of the small, square boxes that he was balancing along with the tray containing our two medium-sized drinks. "One personal pan ham and cheese pizza for you." He then eyed his iced caramel cappuccino I had finished off. "By the looks of it, you don't need this root beer."

I nearly leaped up for the drink. "Yes, I do!"

He laughed softly as he handed me my soda. "Since I'm such a nice guy, I'll give you a drink." He sat down next to me and opened up his pizza box. The smell of freshly cooked vegetables on a melted cheese pizza drifted through the air.

I carefully ate a slice of pizza and gulped my root beer. "So, what do you want for Christmas, Eddie?" I asked.

He finished off his slice before answering me with a nonchalant shrug. "I don't care. Whatever you give me will be fine, Shelly."

I rolled my eyes at him. "Thanks for being so specific. This is exactly what you told me last Christmas."

Eddie set down his pizza box and looked over at me. "Well, we weren't dating then. Now you know me better." He then retracted his fangs and gave me a loving kiss on my pizza-flavored lips. "Any gift you give me will be wonderful," he whispered in my ear, once he was done kissing.

I gently pulled away from him. "Well, at least, I know what I want for Christmas."

"And what's that, babe?"

"Well, there are two things I really want: either, a digital camera or a new easel with a complete set of colored pencils."

I yawned, suddenly realizing how tired I was. According to my watch, I had another five hours to go before the doll went on sale. I excused myself to use the restroom. When I came back, I finished the rest of my supper as Eddie and I talked about our Christmas plans.

"You sound tired, babe," my boyfriend told me. He picked up our empty containers and dumped them into a nearby trash can. Once he was sitting again, he slipped his arm around me and pulled me close. "Get some sleep. I'll wake you up around eleven-thirty."

I leaned my head against his shoulder and shut my eyes. My mind blocked out the commotion around us, and soon I fell into a deep sleep.

Chapter Five:
Cat Fight! Round One!

"Shelly!" I felt someone gently shake my shoulder.

I opened my eyes, remembering I had fallen asleep against Eddie. "What time is it?" I asked him as I rubbed the sleep from my blue eyes with the palms of my hands.

"Eleven-thirty," my vampire answered as he got to his feet. He pulled me to my feet. He stretched his arms and shook his legs which had fallen asleep.

I nearly collapsed as Eddie grabbed me. "It's okay," I assured him after reading the concern in his eyes. "My butt and legs fell asleep." With the vampire holding me, I was able to shake away the numbness within a few minutes. "So, what did you do to pass the time?"

"Made a few phone calls. Dirk's helping Lisa move. I told them we could help if we got back in time."

"Move?" I said. Then I remembered my best friend, Lisa

Miller, was in the process of moving out of the house we shared. Lisa had her eye on this nice, retro studio apartment with rent I could barely afford on my salary. But Lisa is a wedding planner for five different weddings and has more money to work with.

"Yeah, he said she finally went with that apartment."

"Wow!" I still do not believe my house is going to be empty again after a year.

He nodded. He glanced at his watch. It read 'quarter 'till midnight. He rubbed his hands together. "Are we ready to buy the creepy Somona doll?" he asked with a strong sarcastic tone in his voice.

"Look, you didn't have to come," I told him after we heard a voice over the intercom telling us that Somona the talking doll would go on sale in fifteen minutes.

"Oh, please! You practically begged me to come."

It took me a minute to consider his point. "I had asked you to join me, but I most definitely did not beg. You can pick up a gift for your nephew, Sammy, while I get the doll."

He shrugged. Technically speaking, eight-year-old Sammy isn't my boyfriend's nephew. He's Eddie's cousin's son. But it's weird to call the kid, "Sammy, my cousin once removed."

The line had finally started moving right after the second voice blared over the PA system, "The time is 12:01, and Somona the talking doll is now on sale!" All of the excited mothers, grandmothers, sisters, and aunts rushed into the Toy Carnival like a herd of stampeding wildebeest high on estrogen. Eddie and I were hustled into the store by the madding crowd and we were separated. Right before I lost sight of my boyfriend, he sent me a telepathic message saying he would meet me at the cash register.

The Toy Carnival was your typical store which sold all the latest fads for youngsters of all ages, including the three-layer high display of Somonas, the creepy, talking doll who was staring out at everyone through the plastic covering of the cardboard box. By the time I got to the front of the quickly disappearing display, there was only one doll left.

Everything went in slow motion as the obnoxious grandmother and I went for it. I could almost hear the theme music from Chariots of Fire playing in my mind. It was a race against time. The old lady knocked the box off the shelf, and it tumbled to the multi-colored polka-dot carpeted floor. Heck, no! I thought to myself as I watched the lady reach for the doll. There was no way I was going to stand in line at another store for another six hours for this stupid doll. Youth and treachery will triumph over old age and skill. Like a hawk, I swooped down and picked up the box before the senior citizen had a chance to even touch the doll a second time.

"Give me that doll!" she screeched.

Now, I could've been compliant and just handed the toy over to her, but I was getting sick, and there was no way in hell I was going to get another Somona doll, if by a slim chance another store was going to sell it. "No!" I told her as I clutched the box to my chest. "I'm sure the store has extras in the back."

The poor satyr sales clerk with the various facial piercings shook his head vigorously. He was wearing the dress code for Toy Carnival: a bright green polo shirt and a pair of black cargo pants over his goat-like legs. Clipped next to his name tag which read, "Hello, my name is Basil," was a ribbon that read, "Please, be patient with me. I'm new." I could tell he was barely sixteen because his two curved horns were just starting to grow out from his head of bushy, blond hair. "N-N-No," he stammered, evidentially afraid of a possible catfight during his first week on the job. "That's the last one we have in stock."

"Maybe we could use some kind of duplicating spell," I suggested, still not willing to give up the doll.

"Duplicating spell!" she spat. "I want the real thing!" She grabbed the end of the box and began to pull.

"Lady," I said, shocked, but still keeping my death grip on the purple and pink flowered box, "I got to it first."

"Give it to me, you young whippersnapper!"

Whippersnapper? Who uses that term anymore? I jerked the box out of her hand as I frantically looked around for my boyfriend for backup. Where had he wandered off to?

What are you doing, Shelly? Eddie asked me subconsciously. He had just rounded the corner with a three-car train set in his arms. He nearly dropped it as he stared in shock witnessing his girlfriend and an elderly woman fight over a doll.

This lady wants Somona, I explained as I gave another yank on the box which was slowly slipping from my grasp, *but I got to it first!*

Just give it to her.

There's no way I'm standing in line to get another doll! She can have it when she pries it from my cold, dead fingers.

Eddie began to back away. The last thing he wanted to get involved in was a fight. He was counting on me to take care of this problem all on my own.

The lady let go of the box, and I breathed a huge sigh of relief, but that was short-lived. I watched in horror as the old Welkie reached into her bag and pulled out one of her long metal knitting needles. She raised it high above her head and literally charged at me with the pointy end heading straight towards me. "Give me that doll, you shrew!" she screamed at me.

That kicked Eddie into gear. He immediately set the train down on an empty shelf and rushed in between us. "Citadel!" he said as a pale green force field encircled around me, preventing the needles from penetrating my skull. Once I was out of harm's way, the force field dissipated, and Eddie stepped in front of me. Then he turned to face the Welkie. "Don't call my girlfriend that name. If you try to hurt her, I will make a personal call to mall security."

She put away the knitting needle and glared at me. "Fine,"

she told me and Eddie. "I'll leave, but you just destroyed my

favorite granddaughter's Christmas!" Before she stomped off,

she said, "I wjeh eej, I njii eej. I wjeh eej, I njii eej. Qhel cxzd ehd

dhoudo mobe gixw eoqw. I wjeh eej, I njii eej."

I looked at Eddie. "What did she just say?"

He shrugged as he picked up the train. "I don't know. I

wasn't paying attention. I was more concerned about the

possibility of you being almost skewered by an old lady's knitting

needles." He shook his head in disbelief. "I can't believe my own

girlfriend was fighting over a doll."

"At least, I got the thing," I said, a little triumphantly, as we

paid for our items. "Annika better be happy."

By the time we were leaving the mall, Lisa had called and

invited Eddie and me to come over and see her new apartment.

We spent about twenty minutes over there, touring her new

place. When we got to my house, Eddie and I sat in the driveway

for a few minutes, kissing each other. Finally, I gave him one last

good-night kiss, gathered up the doll and my purse, and went into my now empty house. I tossed the doll and my purse on the kitchen table. I was about to head off to the bathroom to get ready for bed when I noticed something out of the corner of my eye. "Did that doll just blink at me?" I asked myself as I faced the toy I had so bravely fought for. The doll just stared back at me with glassy, blank eyes. "No, Shelly," I told myself, "it's just a doll. It can't come to life. The AA batteries aren't even in yet." I shrugged it off and went to bed.

In hindsight, I should've given the lady the dumb doll.

Chapter Six:
The Doll Comes Alive

When I walked into my kitchen the next morning, I noticed three things. First, I had the worst headache ever, and I felt like someone had shoved several cotton balls up my nostrils. The second thing I noticed was the box was in the middle of the table on its side. "Strange," I said aloud to myself. "I thought I set the box on the edge of the table. Maybe, Lisa moved it." Then it hit me, the third thing I noticed was Lisa's absence. Lisa had moved into her new apartment last night or early this morning. I shook my head. Maybe she had come in to grab something she had forgotten and knocked the box over.

I went into the bathroom and went through the medicine cabinet above my toilet until I found a box of cold and cough medicine. Okay, it had expired a couple of years ago, but the medicine was probably still good. I popped the recommended dosage into my mouth before getting ready for the day.

When I stepped back into the kitchen, the box was upright. I stared at it in shock. There was no way the box could be standing because I hadn't even touched it. "How did that happen?" I asked the doll, and then realized I was talking to an inanimate object. I needed to get out of the house and do some Christmas shopping. As I was about to leave the house, I turned and looked at the doll. It seemed as if the corners of its mouth had turned into a sadistic smile. "It's not alive," I told myself, "It's not alive."

I took my winged horse, Jordan, over to Randall's, a discount department store in hopes of finding the perfect Christmas gift for Eddie. After scouring the aisles for something my boyfriend might like, I gave up trying and swung by the home décor section and picked out a pumpkin-spiced candle set to give Lisa as a housewarming gift.

About thirty minutes later, I found myself sitting in Lisa's kitchen drinking a cup of mint-flavored coffee. Lisa had her bleach-blonde hair up in a ponytail under a red and green bandana. She is a year older than me but has always acted very mature for her age. "Shelly, I like the candles. I'll have to light them the next time Dirk comes over," she said with a smile. "Then he'll think that I made him something to eat."

I nodded. "Well, you liked them the last time we were in the store." I took another sip of the coffee. Then I remembered what I had seen this morning. "Did you come back to my place at all last night?"

She shook her head. "No, why?"

I told her what had happened with the doll. "It's just a little strange."

Lisa was clearly having trouble believing me. She wasn't trying to hide her skepticism in her green eyes. "Shelly," she asked slowly, as if not wanting to upset me, "are you sure that the doll did move? You may have been more tired with all that happened last night."

"No, I'm positive I saw the doll move."

"But you said the medicine you took had expired."

I tried to argue with her, but then I remembered the movie conversation I had with Eddie. Lisa was right. There was no way that the doll could have moved. I dropped the subject, and I had a sudden idea. Perhaps Lisa could give me some ideas for Eddie's gift. "What are you getting Dirk for Christmas?" I asked.

"I went online and bought some of the original albums of Dirk's first rock band."

"Oh, he's going to love that." When Dirk first became a vampire, he had started a semi-famous band called the Coffin Bangers. They sang the same style of music as the Beach Boys, but it was nothing to write home about.

"So, what are you giving Eddie?"

"I haven't got a clue. I mean, he's got everything he needs."

Lisa thought for a moment. "I've got it. Why don't you get him some cologne?"

"Nah, one of his old colleagues from when he worked with the Agency sent him a complimentary box of Blue Ice. He has about six bottles of it."

"What about getting him a pair of motorcycle gloves?"

I thought it over for a few minutes. "Okay, that sounds good. Eddie could always use a new pair of gloves, but I want to get him something more. This is going to be our first Christmas as a couple, and I want to get him something very special."

Lisa offered me another cup of coffee, and I declined it. She furrowed her brow in thought as she began to peel off the skin of an orange she retrieved from her fridge. "You know what Dirk told me the other night."

"No, what?"

"He said Eddie mentioned to him how much he loved your paintings."

I had to think about that for a minute or so. Lisa was right. Eddie did care a lot about my artwork. We had nearly been killed over some of my paintings. Come to think of it, I had never given him one of my paintings. "You're a genius, Lisa," I told her as I gave her a huge hug of thanks. "I'm going to paint a picture of Eddie with his motorcycle. He'll love it."

When I got home a few hours later, I was immediately freaked out by the doll box that was now lying on the floor. "I'm not going crazy," I told myself as I scooped up the ugly doll. It gave me the creeps just looking at it so I placed it face down on the table. To calm my semi-shattered nerves, I threw my spring jacket over the box. Out of sight, out of mind.

I then walked over to the closet right next to my bedroom door. Pushing aside the few dresses and skirts I own (including the royal blue bridesmaid gown I was going to wear at my father's wedding), I found a box full of pictures I had taken over the past six years. There were photos of Dad refurnishing the diner, holidays and various outings with him and Amelia, and many more photos. I began to sift through all the photos, picking out the ones that weren't out of focus, had red eyes, or were just plain awful. I began to slowly realize I had no pictures of Eddie's motorcycle. How was I going to paint my boyfriend's Christmas present if I had no pictures of his favorite mode of transportation? I would have to get some pictures without his knowledge.

It was about a half hour later when I glanced up to hear knocking coming from the kitchen. I jumped in terror, thinking might have been the doll when I realized who was making the noise. "Door's unlocked!" I called out.

My brother, Robin, came into my house. He was still wearing his blue police uniform, even though he was off-duty. Robin is a year older than me. He and I have the same deep blue eyes, but his hair is more auburn-colored than mine. When he was younger, he was a good deal shorter than me, but now he's as tall as my father. "Shelly," he called from the kitchen, "are you coming anytime soon? Dad's waiting for us!"

"Just a minute, Robin!" I called back to him. "I'm just about done with this pile of pictures." I looked over at the four piles of photos that had accumulated on the pale green living room carpet. "Why are you picking me up? Eddie said he was going to."

"Dad volunteered him to help lug in the Christmas tree stand."

No surprise there. The mandatory volunteer thing was typical of my father. I was just glad I wasn't carrying in the stand like last year. That thing was a three-inch thick piece of five-by-five plywood covered in a thin layer of red velvet which did nothing to protect your hands from getting an array of splinters. Not only was the base awkward to carry, but the stand itself was made from twenty pounds of green Flexi-steel, a metal stronger than regular steel, but flexible enough to be shaped into any form. And believe me, carrying it is like lugging elephants around. According to Amelia, in a moment of madness, Dad had bought the stand at a yard sale a couple of years ago. Unfortunately, she hasn't been able to convince my father to get a lighter one.

"I'm almost done, Robin." I quickly finished looking through the pill in my hands and then realized I had a huge stain on the front of my shirt. "Okay, let me change my shirt." I went into my bedroom and threw on a green and purple striped sweater. "Hey, Robin," I called through the closed door, "can I borrow your camera pen?"

"Why?"

"I need it for Eddie's Christmas present."

"You're not going to do anything illegal with my camera this time, are you? Because the last time I lent it to you, the photos were confiscated as evidence."

"Oh, come on. Don't you trust your own sister?"

I heard a snort of disbelief. After a few long seconds, he

replied, "Fine, I'll let you borrow it. Just don't do anything illegal."

I came out of my bedroom. "Who, me?" I asked innocently. I saw him peeking under the jacket on my table.

"Holy crap!" he screamed the second he saw the butt ugly doll. "Eddie was right. This thing is hideous!" He looked at me in disbelief. "You fought over this thing?"

"Hey," I protested, "it was the last doll in the store." I grabbed the jacket and covered the doll back up with a spare towel. There was no way I was going to tell Robin I had seen the doll move. No need to become the unwitting butt of his jokes.

"Come on, let's get going. I want to enjoy the fact Eddie lent me his car."

"Which one?" I grabbed my purse and locked up the house as I began to follow my brother out the door.

"The carrot car."

I was going to have a little talk with Eddie. "Oh, that's not right. He won't even let me sit behind the steering wheel, much less drive it."

"It's a guy thing, Shelly. Plus, I got out of helping to lug in that tree stand. He even said I could use his car to pick up

Brooke for Dad and Amelia's wedding. The car is a genuine

chick magnet."

I rolled my eyes at my brother. Through the window in the

front door, something on the kitchen table caught my eye. Did

the towel just move? Nah, I thought to myself as I climbed into

the passenger seat, my eyes must be playing tricks on me.

Robin, grinning, slid behind the steering wheel. "This is so

cool!" He inserted the key into the ignition. A few moments later,

we were speeding down the road to our father's restaurant.

My father's diner can seat about one hundred people. It's

a fifties-style diner with its black-and-white checkered linoleum

floor and retro red tables and chairs but has the atmosphere of a

sports dinner with the light bouncing off the pale yellow walls.

There are even matching booths in three of the four corners of

the large restaurant. The fourth corner of the room, only a few

steps away from the kitchen doors and my dad's back office is

where Eddie serves ice cream.

Instead of serving alcohol in the diner, Dad installed an ice

cream counter. After seeing the negative effects of alcohol during his twenty-some-odd-year career as a police officer, Dad decided it was best not to serve any when he opened up the diner. Everyone has said that this is a great idea because what better way to drown your sorrows than in a bowl of ice cream?

Today the diner was closed, but the lights were still on. Some of the staff were decorating for the holidays. It was a bit early, but next week Dad and Amelia were going to be on their honeymoon.

Robin and I walked in the unlocked back door, through the kitchen, and into the main dining area. Dad was standing near the ice cream counter with his fiancée. "Amelia, how about we put it near the window this year?" he asked her.

Forty-three-year-old Amelia Cross placed a nicely manicured hand on my father's shoulder. She is human, just like my family. "Timothy, dear, just pick a place so Eddie and Bruce can set the stand down."

Struggling under the weight of the stand was Eddie and my dad's best friend, forty-five-year-old Bruce Miller. He used to be my dad's partner on the police force but now is the head cook at the diner. "Timothy," he growled just under his breath, "if you don't pick a spot in the next three seconds, I will throw this stand at you."

Eddie doesn't always agree with Bruce, but this time he does. "He's right, Mr. Anderson. This thing is really heavy."

I took one look around the diner as I popped a strawberry-flavored cough drop into my mouth. The jukebox near the bathrooms had been removed so the tree could be put in its normal place. "Here's a novel idea, Dad," I said. "Why don't you put the tree where we had it last year?"

Amelia threw her hands up in the air. "That's what I've been telling him," she said, shaking her head of short, black hair at Dad.

Dad looked at her with his baby blue eyes and finally gave in. "Bruce, you and Eddie can set the stand down where the jukebox was."

Both Eddie and Bruce breathed a huge sigh of relief as they set the stand down. Eddie stood up and rubbed his shoulder. He came over and gave me a quick kiss on the lips. "Hey, babe," he said. "Sorry about not picking you up. Your dad volunteered me to carry that thing down from the rooftop storage shed."

"No problem," I replied, so glad I wasn't recruited for the job "And just to quell your fears, the car's fine."

"Hey, Eddie," Robin called. "Let's go lug in the tree!"

"Sure," he said as he followed my brother out the back door.

I noticed that the three totes of Christmas decorations had been already placed behind the ice cream counter. Amelia and I opened the box labeled Christmas lights and pulled out a new box of miniature, clear bulbs. "So, are you all ready for the wedding?" I asked her.

She smiled at me. "Of course, Shelly." She used her telekinesis to unravel the string of lights as I helped stretch out the lights. Then she said in a low voice so Dad wouldn't hear. "I think your father is getting a little nervous though." She was about to say something else when we heard Eddie and Robin shouting for someone to open the back doors. Once again, she used her mind to open the doors, and in walked my brother carrying the trunk of the seven-foot pine tree up on his shoulder, leaving a trail of needles in their wake.

Eddie was carrying the top of the tree, trying not to get poked in the eye with one of the tree branches. As he and Robin began carefully setting the tree in the base, his cell phone, sitting on the countertop, started to ring to the tune of "I'm a Believer." I recognized that ring, and so did everyone else as they all looked at me. "Shelly, why are you calling my cell? You're right here." the vampire asked.

I glanced over at the caller ID before answering Eddie's phone. It was my cell phone, but I certainly wasn't calling him.

"Shell," Eddie asked me, "you want to answer it?"

"Hello?" I said into the phone, unsure of who was going to be on the other end of the line. "Hello?" I said again after no answer.

Eddie grabbed the phone from me. "Hello! Hello!" he finally hung up a few seconds later. "Is this some kind of joke, Shelly?" he asked me.

"No! If it was, it would be a really lame joke." I looked around in my purse for my phone. "Oh, crap!" I said after an intensive search.

"What's wrong, Shelly?" Dad asked.

"My cell phone's not with me," I replied.

"Well, you and Eddie hash this out while the rest of us decorate the diner," Dad said to me as he and Bruce began to tighten the stand's screws into the trunk of the tree.

Eddie and I sat down at a nearby table. "Okay," he said, "let's try calling your cell phone so that we can figure out what's going on." He had an idea of what might be going on. "I bet it's Fern. She's probably making crank phone calls."

Fern Van Helsing was not only a ghost, but Eddie's sister who liked to pull practical jokes once in a while. This was a stretch, even for her. "You sure?" I asked him.

He gave a confident nod before dialing my cell phone number. We listened as it rang twice before someone picked it up. "Hello," Eddie said.

No answer.

"Hello."

Still no answer.

"Come on, Fern. We know it's you. Just—." He couldn't finish his sentence because the line went dead. "She hung up," he said. "She'll probably confess later on tonight."

"Okay," I said, still not convinced Fern was the one who called. But was I going to tell my boyfriend who I thought might have made the call? Yeah, sure. Everyone will believe a doll decided to make crank calls.

"Hey, Shelly," Robin said, "you might want to be careful."

"Why?" I asked as Eddie and I got up from our seats.

"Because there have been a string of home invasions," he replied. He handed Amelia a box of ornaments before leaping over the counter. "These robberies have been more of a smash-and-grab than anything else."

"I appreciate the fact that you're looking out for me, but how do these robberies apply to me?" I asked.

"The thieves target houses with the numbers 'eight' and 'zero' in the street number. I'm telling you this because I want you to be careful, Shelly," Robin said as he and I began to wrap the tree with a seven-foot-long string of gold garland.

"I'm always careful!" I said.

Eddie, who was placing the hooks on the red, blue, and gold ornaments, snorted in disbelief. He knows me very well. I try to be careful, and it's not like I purposely try to get myself into trouble. Of course, my boyfriend's not one to buy that.

"Your brother's just looking out for you, Shelly," Dad reminded me. He plugged the string of lights into the outlet, and the entire diner went black. "Hey, Bruce!" he yelled out in the darkness.

"Got it," Bruce said. We all could see the brilliant stream of electricity leap from his fingers into the light socket. Within moments the room lit up. You see, Bruce can control, generate, and absorb electrical fields. It's really useful when the lights go out, but you don't want to get him angry. His fiery red hair and his electrokinesis create a bad combination with his short temper. He stood up and put his hands on his hips. "Do you need me anymore, Timothy?" he asked.

"Nope, I think we're all set, Bruce," Dad replied as he helped Robin and me with the rest of the garland.

"Good," Bruce replied, "because I told Libby I would meet her at her place fifteen minutes ago." He waved goodbye to us and left the diner.

Amelia looked at my father. "I really hope Bruce marries Libby. She's the only one who can calm him down when his temper flares up."

"Let's concentrate on one wedding at a time, dear," Dad told her. He came up behind Amelia and wrapped his arms around her waist, not once, but twice. Then he stretched his neck around and kissed her on the lips. I know this is hard to imagine, but my father can stretch himself without hurting his body.

"Dad," Robin said with a semi-sick look on his face, "you're not going to do that at the wedding, are you?"

"What? Kiss Amelia?" Dad asked as he and his future bride stopped kissing.

"No, that thing you just did with your body. It's weird," Robin replied as he brought the tree to its greenest using his chlorokenesis.

Dad was about to protest when Amelia shot him down with one look. "He's right, honey. It's okay in private, but not in public."

Dad shrugged his shoulders. "I'll stop."

For the rest of the night, we decorated the restaurant for Christmas while listening to festive music. Eddie dropped me off at my house and drove away after I got inside. And that's when things started to get freaky.

When I got inside, I found my cell phone on the table. I decided to check out the dialed calls. Somehow my phone had called Eddie without me touching it. I needed to talk to Fern.

As if on cue, the forever eighteen-year-old ghost appeared in my kitchen. "What's up?" she asked me. She looks a lot like her brother with her long, curly black hair and green eyes. She became a ghost the same night Eddie was turned into a vampire.

"Did you use my cell phone to call Eddie earlier today?" I asked her.

"No! I was with friends all night. I came by to ask if I could borrow one of your card games."

"Sure," I said as I tried to figure out what was going on while Fern went through the bookcase where I kept my board games. Just by reading the ghost's mind, I knew for a fact she was telling the truth. Okay, so if she didn't make the call, then who did?

I glanced over at the pile on my table. No, no, the doll couldn't have made the phone call. I needed to get rid of that thing. Still covering the box with the towel, I scooped it up and stuffed it into the back of the closet's top shelf. For some reason, that doll was making my flesh creep, and not just because it was ugly. There was something weird about Somona, the talking doll.

Chapter Seven:
A False Alarm

Nothing unusual happened for the next two days. A good

thing because the expired cold medicine was making my head

and nose feel like they were going to explode. I needed to buy

some new medicine, or I would be blowing my nose or hacking

up a lung during Dad's wedding ceremony.

After work, I picked up some cold medicine and

returned home with Christmas on my mind. It was the time of

year to put up my pre-lit, artificial Christmas tree. As I was

getting the box of ornaments from my closet, I let out a

short-lived scream of horror. On the floor was an empty flowered

box. I don't know which scared me more: the doll-size hole that

had been cut out of the plastic window or one of my red-handled

paring knives that was lying at the bottom of the box. Oh, did I

mention the doll was nowhere to be seen? I did a frantic search through the closet, pushing aside boxes of photos, clothes, and random junk, until I found the doll at the very back.

It was wearing a very menacing smile. I shivered involuntarily as I removed the knife from the box and replaced it with the doll. How was I going to tell Creighton about the hole in the box? "Oh, by the way, your niece's doll came alive and stole a paring knife from my kitchen drawer so it could cut a hole in the box." Then it would be off to the padded rooms for me.

I slammed the closet door and went up to the loft to get my Christmas tree out of its storage box. After putting on some festive music, it took me about fifteen minutes to set the tree up and plug in the lights. Half of the bulbs were out. I shook my head in disgust. Next year there would have to be a new, fake Christmas tree in my home. I found myself glancing nervously towards the closet. "Shelly," I told myself, "you are getting paranoid." I needed some company.

Eddie came over in a few minutes in his racing car. It had snowed a good three inches the night before, and so I was surprised he still hadn't fixed his picklemobile. There was no trace of car grease on his hands. That didn't surprise me because he has a special kind of soap that can remove anything from your hands. He threw his jean jacket over the back of a dining room chair. "So, what can I do?" he asked me.

I tossed him a spool of thick silver ribbon. "First, we are going to wrap the ribbon around the tree."

"Got it," he said as he took off the rubber band I had placed around the spool. It shot off his fingers and hit me in the left temple. The vampire gasped. "Are you okay, babe? I'm so sorry!"

I rubbed my temple. "It's okay, hon," I told him. "But maybe I should take off the rubber bands."

"Sounds like a good idea," he said as he unwound the ribbon and began to gently wrap it around my six-foot-tall tree. By the time he was done, the tree looked very gorgeous but still needed another roll of ribbon.

"Oh, guess what?" I said as I started to unwrap a roll of royal blue velvet ribbon. Not giving my boyfriend enough time to answer, I continued. "I went out and bought a scrapbook for Dad and Amelia's gift. Want to see it?"

Eddie gave a huge sigh of relief, grateful I hadn't dragged him into any craft stores. "Sure, why not," he replied.

I handed him the ribbon spool and went over to the kitchen table where I had placed a plastic bag. I took out a soft blue and cream striped, ten-page scrapbook and showed it to Eddie. "See, isn't it pretty?"

"Yeah," he said as I flipped through the blank pages, "You know what would look nice? A little, engraved plaque on the front."

"Yeah, that would look great."

"Then after that, we just need to throw a few pictures on each page, and we'll be done."

"Not quite," I said as I pulled out a package of specialized scrapbook paper, stickers, and other essential scrapbooking materials. "We also need these."

"Crap," he muttered, realizing there was no easy way out for him.

I was about to remind him this gift was from both of us and that he needed to do his share when I heard a thump coming from the closet. I let out a short, horrified gasp.

Eddie noticed the scared look on my face. "You okay, Shell?" he asked.

"I'm fine," I lied. I jumped again when we heard a second thud. "Okay, I'm kind of scared right now. Can you check out the closet?"

Eddie raised a skeptical eyebrow at me. "Aren't you a little old to believe in closet monsters?"

I knew he was going to have a hard time believing me, but I told him anyway. "It's the doll!" I replied, not believing the words that tumbled out of my mouth.

"The doll?"

I told him what was going on with the doll. "I think it's alive!"

"Shelly, I highly doubt—."

I cut him off. "Can you at least check it out? What harm could it do?"

He threw up his hands in defeat and walked to the closet. With a flourish, he threw the door open. "See, the doll's on the floor."

I peeked timidly over his shoulder. "That's not possible! I

just put it up on the shelf."

"Are you sure?"

"Yes, I know I did."

Eddie picked up the doll. "See, it's harmless. I can sense no magic in—." He stopped short as the doll reached for his throat. "Oh, no! It's got me!" he shouted in terror.

I was about to scream in horror when I read his mind. "That's not funny, Edgar Van Helsing!" I snapped, using his full name.

"Oh! Come on, Shelly, lighten up," he said as he removed the doll's hand from his Adam's apple. "It was just a joke."

I crossed my arms and glared at him. "That wasn't funny. I really thought—."

"That the doll attacked me?" he said as he put it back on the top shelf and shut the door. "There is no magic connected to it. It isn't alive."

"Then how do you explain the paring knife at the bottom of the box?"

Eddie leaned against the doorframe of my bedroom with his arms crossed. "Bad marketing idea?"

I glowered at him. "Be serious, Eddie. That doll is alive."

"Are you sure your eyes weren't playing tricks on you?"

"I'm positive. I've seen the doll move. Why won't you believe me?"

"Shelly."

"You said so yourself. Inanimate objects can come alive."

"Yeah, but that's ancient magic. Nobody uses it anymore." He came over and ran his fingers through my hair, which he knows I love. He finally realized that his little prank had really scared me. "I'm really sorry about my joke, babe. I shouldn't have scared you like that." He then turned me around and wrapped his arms around my waist. "Will you forgive me?" He leaned his head on my shoulder.

This sweet gesture caused me to melt into his arms. I reached up and gently stroked his jaw with the palm of my hand. "Of course, I forgive you."

"Good, because Christmas isn't a great time to be in the doghouse." Even though Eddie was having trouble believing me, he wasn't going to push the issue any further. It's one of the things I love about him.

I wriggled out of his embrace. "Let's go finish the tree," I said as I pulled him towards the kitchen. With both of us in festive moods, we finished my tree and enjoyed a couple of rounds of eggnog.

In the middle of the night, I was thrown awake by the sound of the television. What was going on? In my groggy state, I tried to remember if I had left the television on. No, I always turn the TV off before going to bed. I felt the pulsing roar in my ears as I remembered what Robin had said about the robberies. Someone had broken into my house and was watching late-night infomercials in my living room. I grabbed my cell phone off my nightstand and dialed the police.

"9-1-1. What is your emergency?" the dispatcher on the other end of the line asked me.

"This is Shelly Anderson on 70 Waverly Way," I said, quietly while struggling to calm the tremor rising in my voice. "Th-th-there's someone in my house!"

"Are you sure, ma'am?"

"Yes, they've turned the television on. I'm in my bedroom."

"Do you know how many people are in your home?"

I pressed my ear against the closed door. Soft, light footsteps could be heard. "At least, one person. I can't tell."

"Miss, stay in your bedroom. I'm sending over a unit right now. Don't hang up."

"Thank you," I said.

I don't know what compelled me to crack open the bedroom door, but it sure scared the crap out of me when I did. Not fully comprehending, much less believing what I saw, the twenty-inch doll leaped up on the couch with the agility of a monkey, took the remote control, and began to flip through the channels. I was probably disappointed I didn't have cable. Then it looked at me and gave me a malicious leer.

My heart started to race faster than a freight train on steroids, and I slammed the door hard.

"Miss?"

Oh, crap. I had forgotten the dispatcher was still on the other end of the line. "Oh, nothing," I lied. This lady would never believe me a doll was channel surfing in my living room. "I think the intruders have gone." I heard knocking on my front door.

"Miss Anderson, it's the police!"

"The police are here," I told the dispatcher before hanging up. I slowly opened my bedroom door, half-expecting the doll to take a flying leap at me. But it didn't. Instead, it stared lifelessly at the blaring television screen, the evil smile wiped clean away from its face, and the remote control at its side. Had I, in a moment of panic, imagined the whole thing? Was I losing it? I had no idea.

The rapid knocking on the front door brought me back to my senses. I threw my sneakers on my bare feet and hurried to open the door.

Two uniformed elves pulled me outside and did a thorough search of my home while I stood there in the cold. My brother's dragon flew down on the driveway. "I came as soon as I heard," Robin said as he lent his coat to keep me warm. "Are you okay, sis?"

"Just scared that's all," I told him as I nodded thanks for the jacket.

"Nothing to report, Sergeant Anderson," one of the officers said. "There's been no forced entry." He looked over at me. "It's safe to go inside."

"Shelly," Robin asked as he got out his notepad and a pen once we were inside, "can you tell me what happened?"

It was at this point I began to babble nervously in front of my brother and his fellow officers. "I woke up to hear the television on. Thinking someone was in the house, I called 911. Then I decided to see who had broken in so I could give you guys a good description of the culprit. When I opened the door, I saw that doll leap up on the couch and start channel surfing," I said breathlessly as I led the police to the living room and pointed to the toy.

My brother gave me the same disbelieving look Eddie had given me earlier that evening. "Okay," he said, putting away his notepad, "let me get this straight. The doll leaped on the couch and was flipping through the channels?"

"Yes!" I said as I nodded vigorously.

"Maybe, it was looking for a good show," remarked one of the officers.

Robin ignored his coworkers and picked up the doll. It lay limp and lifeless in his hands. He shook it a couple of times.

Nothing happened. "Are you sure you didn't leave the television on?"

"The doll turned it on, honestly!"

Robin told the officers he could handle the rest. Once the others were gone, he turned to look at me. "Shelly, it's late. You know what Dad would say to this. That you've let your imagination run wild."

"Robin Daniel Anderson," I growled as I placed my hands on my hips."For one thing, I'm an adult, and secondly, I'm not making this up!"

He shrugged helplessly just as his walkie-talkie blared something about a 10-53 on Northern. "Look, sis, I've got to go. I think you're overstressed with Dad's upcoming wedding and everything. Just get some rest." He waved goodbye and walked out the door, leaving me alone with the doll.

I needed to take care of this doll once and for all. I stuffed the doll back inside the box and then wrapped it in three layers of Saran Wrap. I rummaged around for a lock-and-seal plastic tote until I found one twice as big as a shoebox. Then I threw the box inside the tote, sealed it, and put it in the very back of my closet.

There was no way the doll could break out of that prison. "Ha," I

told the toy, "try getting out of that."

Chapter Eight:
I Lose and Learn Something Very Important

Despite the fact the Chucky doll was in a secure tote in my closet, I didn't sleep well for the rest of the night. By the time my alarm clock went off at 6:30 the next morning, I had gotten about two hours of sleep since I had called the police.

Once I arrived at work, I had made up my mind to prove to everyone, including myself, that I wasn't going crazy. The doll was alive because of some reasonable explanation. Perhaps there was a defect that caused the dolls to come alive. I was determined to find out the reason by calling the company directly.

Then again, I could've been experiencing hallucinations from the old cold medicine I had taken. The sore throat and coughing had finally gone away. Maybe I was just experiencing the side effects. As I went online during my fifteen-minute break,

I jotted down both the drug company's and the toy company's phone numbers for questions and complaints.

After lunch, I made the first phone call to the Toy Carnival. After spending about ten minutes feeling like a volleyball being passed back and forth to different departments, I finally talked with a real-live person. "Hello, I bought a Somona doll about a week ago. I was wondering if there have been any complaints about the doll. Like it moving on its own without batteries?" Man, I felt like an idiot, asking if anyone had complained about evil dolls.

"No, ma'am," the sales representative on the other end of the line replied. We haven't heard any complaints about the doll. But if you are dissatisfied with it, you can send it back or drop it off at any one of our stores, and we will send you a new doll free of charge."

Why would I want another creepy doll? "Uh, no thank you, but thanks anyway." I hung up the phone with a glum look on my face. Okay, maybe I was seeing things.

The call to the drug company was pretty much the same thing. They were pretty adamant that their medicine didn't cause hallucinations. I began to suspect they were more concerned about a possible lawsuit than the health of their consumers.

I sat back in the faded pink leather armchair in the staff room. I couldn't believe I had reached a dead end. Was I experiencing side effects of the expired medication or was the doll really alive? If it was alive, then how did it come alive?

Then I remembered what Eddie had told me about the ancient spell that could bring objects to life. Who could have cast that kind of spell on the doll? And what spell was it? Using my librarian "superpowers," I went on the Internet to find any kind of magic spells that can bring objects to life. It took me almost to the end of my lunch break, but I finally found an obscure website about ancient spells, such as love potions, hair growth elixirs, and turning princes into frogs and turning them back again.

Finally, I found what I was looking for. A Life Curse when spoken towards an inanimate object would cause it to come to life. The spell was written in an ancient language, but, fortunately, was translated into the following, "I command you, I compel you. I command you, I compel you. Come alive and bring evil/good upon (insert the name of the person you want to curse.) I command you. I compel you." Well, that certainly didn't sound good. It sounded like this spell could seriously go the way of black magic. One question was possibly answered, but many more arose. Who knew that curse, and why was I their target? I printed off the information to show Eddie.

It was Thursday night, and that meant it was movie and pizza night at Eddie's. Or it would have been if I hadn't suggested we work on Dad and Amelia's wedding present. While I waited for Eddie to pick me up at my house, I began to pack up the crafting supplies along with Robin's pen camera. I figured this could be my chance to sneak in a few pictures for Eddie's painting.

I had bought a ten-pack of decorative scissors (the ones with the curved blades), a packet of assorted paper, acid-free photo mounts, a small paper trimmer, specialized scrapbooking tape, and various embellishments. As I began to put the items and the photos I had picked out in my green canvas bag, I accidentally knocked my purse onto the floor, scattering the contents everywhere. I stopped what I was doing and began to put my keys, wallet, aspirin, and cell phone back into my purse.

That's when I noticed something was missing. I unzipped the pocket where I kept my mother's engagement ring. "Oh, no!" I cried aloud as I stared into the empty pocket. I began to search the floor, seeing if the black ring box had skirted under my refrigerator, table, or pantry. For the next fifteen frantic minutes, I searched without luck. I was down on my hands and knees when I heard the front door open.

"Shell? Are you ready to go?" Eddie asked as he let himself in. I had been smart and had given him a spare key.

I shook my head. "No, I can't find my mom's engagement ring."

My vampire joined me on his knees. Another thirty minutes went by as we nearly turned the whole house upside down. "Are you sure it's not in your purse?"

I nodded, almost on the verge of tears. I couldn't believe I had lost the ring right before Dad's wedding.

"When was the last time you saw it?"

"Eddie, I have to find it! It's the only memento I have of her!"

He placed his hands on my shoulder. "Calm down, babe. When was the last time you saw it?"

"At the mall when I showed it to you."

"And did you put it back in your purse?"

"Yes," I replied, but now I was unsure. I was tired that night, so maybe it fell out. "I think so anyway."

"Why don't you call the mall to see if someone turned it in?"

I wiped away a few remaining tears as I grabbed my phonebook from its usual place, on top of the fridge. Once I found the number to the Moonlight Mall, I called asking if anyone had turned in an engagement ring. No one had turned in anything even close.

Eddie gave me a loving hug. He knew how much the ring meant to me. "It'll turn up, babe," he assured me. "Don't worry about it."

"I'll try."

He kissed me lightly on the cheek. Then he grabbed my canvas bag. "I'll meet you out in the car."

"Okay, I'll be right out. Let me use the bathroom."

Afterward, I gave another glance around the kitchen. "Where is that ring?" I asked aloud. As if in response, I heard an evil chuckle coming from the closet. Then I knew who stole the ring.

"The doll?" Eddie asked me again as we walked into his kitchen. Technically, it isn't his house. He shares it with his brother. I found it odd that we went into his house through the front door, not the side door connected to his garage as we usually do. He set the canvas bag on the table and got out a carton of light eggnog. "Want some?" he asked.

"Sure. Eddie, I'm serious," I insisted. "The doll stole the ring!" I got the supplies out of the bag and began to spread them on the table.

"Why? Because it's out to get you?" Eddie handed me a glass of eggnog as we sat down at the table. "That doesn't make any sense."

"I know it doesn't make any sense. But that doll is pure evil."

"And you know this how?"

"Because I heard it gave me an evil chuckle."

Eddie raised an eyebrow as he took a sip of his egg nog. "Babe—," he started to say but gave up realizing that nothing he said would change my mind. Finally, he changed the subject as he started to look through the pictures. "I see you arranged the photos in what I'm guessing to be chronological order with each date in a separate Zippy Lock bag."

I was more than willing to do a subject change at this point. Eddie was right. I was carrying things a bit too far with this doll thing. "Yep," I opened the package of paper. "Here, help me pick out a nice background for the set of their first date. Dad took Amelia out to Ambrosia and the theater."

"How about a nice white background?"

I rolled my eyes. "No, because it would look boring." I studied the first picture. Dad was wearing a black suit with a red dress shirt and a black tie while Amelia was wearing a black cocktail dress. I had taken the picture right before they had left on their date. I skimmed through the pack of paper until I found a red and black striped one. "Got one." I opened up the first page of the journal and slid the paper in the sleeve.

"Nice picture of them kissing. Who took that one?"

I smiled as I took the picture from Eddie. "Me. Took it from an upstairs window when Dad dropped Amelia off." I began to arrange the pictures on the page and asked for Eddie's suggestion.

"Looks fine, Shell," he said just to appease me.

"Good," I said as I handed him a box of photo mounts.

"Just stick them on the edge of the corner of each picture."

He began to work when we both heard voices coming towards the kitchen.

"You are getting a new suit, Dirk!" Lisa insisted as she and Eddie's older brother came into the kitchen.

"My suits are fine," Dirk protested. He had his shoulder-length, black hair pulled back in a ponytail. "I don't need another one." Then his green eyes scanned the table covered in scrapbooking supplies. "What are you doing, Eddie?" he asked.

"What does it look like?" my boyfriend replied as he attempted to peel the extra photo mount off his fingertips.

"It looks like you've finally lost your manhood."

Eddie and I exchanged glances and rolled our eyes. "I'm pretty secure in my manhood, Dirk," my boyfriend said. "I'm helping Shelly."

"You're not just helping me!" I said to him, "This is our gift to Dad and Amelia." I shot Eddie a dirty look.

"Oh, Shelly, that's a great idea," Lisa said as she began flipping through the scrapbook.

"It's better than that dumb espresso machine we got them," Dirk mumbled, still upset over the fact he had to buy a new suit.

"That's it!" Lisa snapped at him. "Not only are we getting you a new suit, but we're getting you new shoes." She knows how to punish him. He hates shopping. She gathered up her pink leather purse and dragged Dirk out towards the front door.

"Oh, come on, cupcake!" Dirk protested.

Eddie and I waved goodbye. Then he grinned at me. "At least, you didn't make me pick out the scrapbook."

"To tell you the truth, I didn't want to hear you complain about going into craft stores."

"I wouldn't have complained!"

I looked at him. "I'm not talking 'verbal', Eddie."

"Ah, the downfall of being madly in love with a telepath," he said with a huge grin.

I smiled at the vampire. "So, what are you wearing to the wedding?"

"I'm not buying a new suit if that's what you're thinking!"

I shrugged. "Just as long as you wear something that compliments my bridesmaid dress, I don't care what you wear."

Eddie pushed back his chair. "I'll run up to my room and get three suits for you to choose from." He hurried out of the kitchen.

I took this opportunity to grab the camera pen out of the bag. While the cat's away, the mouse will play. This was a perfect chance to take some pictures of Eddie's motorcycle. I made my way to the garage door and tried to turn the doorknob. It was locked. Odd, why would Eddie keep the door locked? Maybe, it was jammed. I tried it again and then a third time. It was locked.

"Ahem!" I heard my boyfriend behind me.

I whirled around, keeping the pen camera hidden from the

vampire. "That was fast!" I said, not explaining why I was trying to unlock the garage door.

Eddie set the charcoal gray, navy, and black suits he had in his arms on the island counter. "Mind telling me what you were doing?" he asked.

I quickly pulled out a lie from my mental fib portfolio. "I heard a weird noise coming from the garage. Did you know that the door's locked?"

Now, it was Eddie's turn to retrieve a fib. "Well, I locked it because your Christmas present's in there." It was a good lie, but he was blocking my telepathy so I couldn't figure out the truth.

"Ooh, can I see it?"

"No! You have to wait until Christmas."

"Oh, come on. Give me a hint!"

Eddie shook his head. "No hints, babe, it'll be a surprise. I can guarantee you that!" he said with a mysterious air.

That was the end of the discussion. For the next couple of hours, we decided on what suit Eddie would wear: the charcoal gray one with a white dress shirt and a royal blue tie. After finishing the scrapbook, we cuddled on the couch as we

watched a B-rated movie. I would have to figure out another way

to take the pictures another time.

Chapter Nine:
I Do Some Breaking and Entering

"I can't believe we're doing this!" Creighton complained as we rode up the street toward the Van Helsing mansion a few days later. The three-story grass-green building stood out against the gray, snowy sky.

"Hey, you owe me one," I told the centaur as I rode on her back. I had called her last night and asked her to take me to Eddie's. I decided to do something a bit drastic to get those pictures. Before leaving my house, I had gotten out the red mini backpack Dad had given me last Christmas and placed the camera pen inside, along with a few other essentials. The backpack was now under my heavy winter coat. Normally, I would have ridden Jordan, but she hates flying in the snow and rain.

"Shelly, I'm surprised you want to keep the doll for a bit longer."

"Well, I thought I could get it specially wrapped for you," I lied. Yeah, more like wrapped in chains and a straight jacket, I thought. I don't like lying to one of my best friends, except when she is about to unwittingly get a demon doll for her niece. "If you don't mind, I'll give you the doll after my dad's wedding."

"No problem. I'd rather keep it at your house because both Annika and Benji have turned my house upside down in search of Christmas presents."

I slid off Creighton's back and trudged in the snow towards the massive attached garage where Eddie keeps his eight cars and one motorcycle and where Dirk keeps his disagreeable dragon, Ringo.

"Okay, Shelly," Creighton said as she reluctantly followed me, "what are you going to do?"

"I need to take pictures of Eddie's motorcycle."

"So, why don't you just ask him to let you take some pictures?"

"What and ruin the surprise? I'm not taking that chance!" I

walked the perimeter of the garage. The building itself is square-shaped with three windows on each side. The front of the garage has two doors which Eddie always locks. The windows are all painted black so neither one of the brothers could get fried by the sun.

I was searching for evidence of a ward. Like most wizards, Eddie and Dirk can put a ward, a protection spell, around their houses. Normally, if someone attempts to break into a Welkie home, they will be literally thrown away by the magical energy of the ward. I made a snowball and threw it up against the gray vinyl siding of the garage. Nothing happened. Eddie normally puts an entire ward around the house and the garage. So, I figured out whose turn it was to put up the ward.

This was going to be easier than I thought. I went around to the back of the garage and spotted a simple, two-pane window. "Okay," I said aloud to myself, "what is under the window inside?" Making a visual image of the garage, I remembered there were some totes full of nuts, bolts, and other car repairing stuff right under the window. It was about a foot higher than I could reach, but I knew someone who could. I dug around in the snow and gravel until I found a softball-size rock.

Using my snowball-throwing abilities, I tossed the rock through the top pane of the window. Shattering glass echoed loudly in the stillness of the late December morning, followed by Creighton's frantic galloping to the back of the garage.

"Shelly," she hissed, "What on earth are you doing?"

"Breaking and entering," I replied nonchalantly. "Boost me up, would you?"

Creighton shook her head as she knelt so I could climb on her back.

I scrambled on and then slowly stood up, using the garage window to balance myself. I carefully slipped my hand through the fresh hole in the window and moved the latch that locked the window to the left. Placing my hands flat on the lower window pane, I pushed the window open.

"I can't believe you're breaking into Eddie's garage," Creighton said as I felt her shift her body. "This kind of behavior is supposed to happen after a bad break-up, and then you break into his house and torch something. What if he catches you?"

I nearly toppled backward, but I caught myself on the

open window ledge. "Stop moving around," I told her. "He

wouldn't. Eddie usually gets up around three. It's only ten o'clock

in the morning. And if he does, I'll make something up." I

attempted to peer into the dark garage. There was a very small

chance I could squeeze through the window. "Hold on to me," I

told her as I took off my winter coat and draped it over her back.

"Okay, I'm going in. Wish me luck!" I pulled myself through the

open window and carefully climbed down the small pile of totes.

Once I was safely on solid ground, I took off my backpack

and retrieved the flashlight that I had brought. The light of the

window cast a dull gray stream of light into the garage. Before

turning the flashlight on, I made note of my surroundings. I was

in the back of the garage. On my right and left were six of

Eddie's vintage cars, each one in the shape of a fruit or a

vegetable. The motorcycle was kept near the front of the

building, along with the carrot car.

With the help of the flashlight, I swiftly headed towards

the front. Past the parsnip-shaped car. Past the corn cob-shaped

one and the zucchini-shaped one. I told you about my

boyfriend's creativity. I didn't see the other car of my affection.

The peanut-shaped car wasn't beside the yellow banana car. Eddie had gotten the peanut-shaped one at a car show a few months ago when he traded his apple-shaped car which looked like a deformed, red box. In addition to the carrot car, I really wanted to take this new car out for a spin.

As I came near the front, I was hit with the overwhelming smell of dragon dung. If you have never encountered dragon dung, consider yourself lucky. It smells like burning sulfur, and this was a very fresh smell. I glanced over at the stable where the rainbow-colored, horse-size dragon was curled up in one of its corners, sleeping soundly. Wisps of blue smoke spewed from his nostrils.

I tiptoed past the stable and headed towards the carrot car and the motorcycle. Something was missing. In the middle of the garage where Eddie does his mechanical work was the peanut car, but the picklemobile was nowhere in sight. I did a couple of sweeps with the flashlight in search of the missing car. I thought Eddie said he was fixing the picklemobile, I said to myself. Then where is it? A thought crossed my mind. Perhaps the thieves Robin had told me about had broken in and stolen the picklemobile. I had the sudden urge to pound on the door leading to the house so I could tell my boyfriend what I had discovered, and then I stopped myself. That would look really great. Eddie would be more suspicious about me breaking into his garage than someone stealing one of his cars.

I walked over to the motorcycle parked near Ringo's stable and took out Robin's pen camera. Aiming the flashlight at the bike, I began snapping pictures at every possible angle. The garage was filled with light every time the flash went off.

Then I heard some movement coming from the stable. I whirled around just in time to see Ringo slowly rising on his hind legs and growling at the same time. I quickly put the camera away in the backpack and slowly began to back away. The dragon let out a menacing snarl before he let out a loud bellow. Fortunately, he isn't the fire-breathing type or I would be crispy right now.

The kitchen door opened up as I darted behind the carrot car. Okay, I hadn't factored in the very real possibility of waking up the temperamental dragon. I flattened myself against the side of the car while I attempted to quiet my labored breathing.

"Ringo, what's wrong, boy?" Dirk asked as he stood in the doorway.

I read his mind and realized that he was going to turn on the garage lights. This gave me time to dart behind a pile of totes by the window. I heard the vampire come down the steps and walk towards the dragon. Dirk was a semi-famous rock star, not an ex-spy like his brother, or he would have done a better search of the garage. He did notice the broken window. "Oh, crap! I'll have to tell Eddie about that." He looked around for a second or two, not seeing what had set Ringo off, and then went back inside, turning off the lights. Once again, the garage was in darkness.

After that close encounter, I hustled out of there. After scrambling up the pile of totes, I leaned out the window. "Creighton!" I hissed.

"Are you okay?" the centaur asked as she helped me out the window.

"Yeah," I said as I closed the window back up, "Ringo nearly gave me away." All that excitement made me hungry. "You want to go grab a bite to eat?"

We went to Anderson's Place for lunch. After we both

ordered the fresh garden salads and diet sodas, Dad came over

to our table. "Shelly, are you okay?" he asked. The familiar look

of concern for my safety was spread across his face.

"Why?" I asked, thinking he had discovered my little

crime. "What's going on?"

"Robin called and said someone had broken into your

house."

"Oh, it was nothing, Dad," I lied. "I thought I heard

someone break in, and I panicked. That's all."

Dad breathed a huge sigh of relief. It was only three days

before the wedding, and the last thing he needed was to be

worried about his only daughter's safety. "That's good to hear.

You guys have a good lunch." He waved bye to us and headed

back to the kitchen.

Once he was gone, I leaned over the table. I had told her

earlier about the false alarm, minus the doll watching television.

"So, what do you think?" I asked the centaur.

"About what?" she asked as she sipped her soda.

"Eddie's missing car. I think someone stole it."

"Maybe he sold it."

I shook my head. "No! He wouldn't sell it. He loves the picklemobile. It was the first car he built. There is no way he would sell the car!"

"Okay, why don't you call Robin to find out if Eddie filed a stolen car report?"

"Tell him what? 'Hey, Robin, I was breaking into Eddie's garage, and I found out someone may have stolen the picklemobile.' I'm sorry, but I don't want to spend my father's wedding day in jail, thank you very much." For the rest of our lunch, we talked about Christmas, the wedding, and Creighton's trip to her grandparents. The question about the missing picklemobile still lingered in the back of my mind.

Chapter Ten:
Another Poor Plan Bites the Dust

I was shelving some nonfiction when I noticed the same old lady I encountered in the toy shop. A thought occurred to me. The doll started acting strangely after the lady and I had fought. She may have cursed the doll by casting a spell or something.

Contrary to popular belief, I don't jump to any kind of conclusions until I know the facts. In this case, I planned to find out one way or the other. She selected some books on complex knitting projects and did not notice me following her as she headed toward the adult circulation desk. I nonchalantly began rearranging books on one of the display tables in the lobby. Now and then, I looked up watching her check out the books she had picked out.

"Five druci in fines!" the lady shouted at Brady, the elfin

clerk behind the check-out desk. "That's not possible! I've returned all my books." I guess the Christmas spirit still hadn't improved her personality.

"Well," Brady said as he turned the computer screen around so the woman could read her library account more clearly, "These fines are from books you brought back late a few weeks ago."

"But I brought those books back!"

"I know you did, but they were returned late, Mrs. Salem."

"Well, I don't have the money to pay for the fines," she snapped angrily.

"That's all right," Brady replied with a huge, patronizing smile as he checked out the books for the Welkie. "You can pay for it later." I watched the Welkie woman gather up her books without so much as a thank you to Brady and storm out the front door.

After she left, I had the perfect opportunity to find out who she was. I looked at her record. She was Myrtle Salem and currently received mail at 737 Highview Lane. I jotted the address on a slip of scrap paper. After work, I was going to pay her a little visit.

It was snowing when I left work for my upcoming confrontation. As I rode Jordan to Highview Lane, I planned my little lecture. Of course, I wasn't going to directly accuse her of possessing the doll, but somehow I was going to get Mrs. Salem to tell me everything. I climbed off my winged horse and walked on the freshly shoveled walkway to the front door of 737 Highview Lane. I rang the doorbell once and shoved my hands into the pockets of my winter jacket. The sun was slowly setting, causing the temperature to drop. I rang the doorbell again.

The door finally swung open, and there stood Mrs. Salem, who immediately recognized me. "You!" she shouted with a pointed finger in my face. "Have you come to ruin some more of my family's Christmas?"

"Look, I grabbed the doll first," I told her.

"Well, are you enjoying the doll?" she sneered at me.

"You cursed that doll somehow, didn't you? I haven't been seeing things. That doll is alive, and you're behind it somehow."

"Are you calling me a witch?"

"Well, if the pointy black hat fits?" I countered.

Mrs. Salem's response was not what I had expected in the least bit. "Duracell!" she snarled as she threw her palms forward in my direction.

Now, this was the first time I had been hit with an energy spell, and it hurt like the Devil. A pinkish ball of energy hit me squarely in the chest, knocking me right into the ornament-filled lawn as I heard the front door slam. I lay on my back surrounded by gentle pink flamingos and little statues of happy lawn gnomes.

Suddenly, everything went haywire. The cute smiles on the lawn gnomes suddenly turned malicious as one of them swung his little trowel at me. I rolled to the left, then to the right, as I barely missed getting impaled by a plastic pink flamingo leg.

Mrs. Salem had done it again. She had brought them to life, and now I was going to be killed by lawn gnomes and pink flamingos. "Kill her! Kill her!" the lawn gnomes began chanting as they raised their gardening tools like actors in a mob scene from Frankenstein.

I managed to scramble to my feet as I whistled for

Jordan. The winged horse spread her wings and flew to my

rescue. She hovered a few feet above, giving me the perfect

chance to grab the saddle horn and pull myself up onto her

back. "Fly, girl, fly!" As we went higher and higher, I glanced

down at the army of lawn ornaments. They seemed to be trying

to follow me, but they couldn't get beyond the white picket fence.

It seemed the objects could go only so far. The spell must have

some kind of geographical perimeter.

I visited Eddie at the diner later that evening. The

wedding was in two days, and fortunately for Dad and Amelia, it

was a slow night. So slow, that when I came in, my boyfriend

was nowhere in sight. The only person in sight was my future

stepmother. She was at Eddie's post behind the ice cream

counter. "Hi, Amelia," I said as I took off my jacket and shook the

snow out of my hair.

"Hello, Shelly," she told me. "Would you like something to

drink?"

"Sure, I'll have a root beer," I said as I set my stuff down

on the counter stool next to me. I was about to ask where my

boyfriend was when I saw Dad talking to him in his office.

Amelia saw him, too, because she immediately closed the door with her mind. "Oh, by the way, Shelly, could you do a quick proofing of the wedding program? I want to make sure that everything is perfect before I send it off to the printers tomorrow." She handed me a copy of the cream-colored program and a pen she retrieved from her pants pocket.

"Uh, sure!" I said, completely taken aback by the sudden closing of the office door. What was going on? "Is Eddie in trouble with Dad?" I asked her as I took a sip of the root beer which she handed me.

"Oh, no!" Amelia assured. She faltered a bit in her speech as if she was trying to come up with an explanation. "There was a shortage in the cash drawer, and they're just trying to figure out what happened."

"Oh!" I said, not completely convinced. If there was a problem with the restaurant's cash drawer, Amelia wouldn't have been trying to hide it from me. No, there was something else going on. I shrugged it off and began checking out the program. Everything was grammar-perfect. The commas, periods, and other punctuation marks were in their right places. So, what was going on? "It looks great, Amelia," I replied as I handed her back the program.

She smiled. "Oh, good, that's one thing off my chest." She frowned at me. "Shelly, I hope you don't mind your father asked Eddie to work tomorrow night during the wedding rehearsal."

"That's okay," I said with a smile. "I'll just make Eddie take me someplace nice."

Eddie came out of the office a few minutes later. "Thanks, Mr. Anderson," he said.

Out of the corner of my eye, I saw Dad smile at my boyfriend. "No problem, Eddie." He went back to the pile of paperwork on his desk.

My boyfriend came over and gave me a peck on the cheek. "Hello, Shell," he said as he switched places with Amelia.

"Hi, Eddie," I told him as I leaned over the counter and returned the kiss.

"Did you get the money situation figured out?" Amelia asked Eddie as she took off her apron.

My boyfriend seemed a little distracted. "Oh, everything's fine," he told her as he quickly blocked his telepathy in my presence.

"Good. I'll just go help your father out with the accounting." Amelia waved goodbye to us and went into the office, closing the door behind her.

Once she was gone, I told Eddie what had happened to me that day. The reaction I got wasn't what I had expected from him. "You accused her of being a witch. That's a pretty harsh accusation."

"But she made the doll come alive," I pointed out.

Eddie rubbed his temples as if to prevent an oncoming migraine which vampires don't get. "You think she brought the doll to life."

I held up my hand to stop him from lecturing as I reached into my purse. I pulled out the printouts of the ancient magic and handed them to my boyfriend. "Look, this magic is possible. Mrs. Salem used this curse to bring the doll to life."

Eddie barely glanced at the papers before folding them back up again and shoving them into the back pocket of his black jeans. Then he leaned on the counter. "Look, Shelly, I have no doubt you were attacked by lawn ornaments." He began chuckling softly when he said that last phrase. Once he regained his composure, he continued, "But you can't go around accusing people of possessing dolls."

"But it makes sense."

"Shelly, I think with everything's that been going on, you've been a little stressed out."

"And you think I must be seeing things?" I was a bit upset Eddie didn't believe me. Maybe he was right. I hadn't heard anything from the closet since Eddie and I did the scrapbook. I decided to change the subject. "Did you pick up the plague for the scrapbook yet?"

"Oh, yeah," he said. He reached under the counter and pulled out a brown paper bag. Opening it up, he handed me a gold plaque about the size of a business card. It had tiny engraved flowers along the edges to match the beautiful calligraphy engraving of Dad and Amelia's names and their wedding date. "So, what do you think?" Eddie asked.

"Wow, honey!" I said, very impressed. "You did a great job. They'll love it." I was putting it back when I saw something else in the bag. "You even got them a card. You're very thoughtful." I took out the card. It was very lovely with a silhouette of a Victorian bride and groom dancing on the front. The message was very sweet talking about how a couple should love each other forever and other typical wedding-type things. I took out a pen from my purse and opened up the card. I addressed it to Dad and Amelia and then signed it from Eddie and me.

"You want to hear something weird?" he asked as he watched me address the envelope.

"Sure," I answered, not looking up from my work. I stuck the card in the envelope sealed it and put it in the bag. "I'll take the card and the plaque with me so that I can finish wrapping their gift."

"Someone broke into my garage yesterday," Eddie said.

"Really?" I asked, feigning surprise.

"Yeah, someone threw a rock through one of the windows. It dented the parsnip car."

So, that's what happened to the rock. Good thing he couldn't read my mind. "Was anything stolen?"

"No. That was the weird thing. I've got a lot of valuables in there." He had decided not to call the police because nothing was stolen, but he did have a very serious conversation with his brother about correctly performing wards.

I checked my watch. I still had to buy wrapping paper for the wedding present. "Look, I've got to go," I told Eddie as I kissed him. "See you on Saturday."

"See you then, Shelly," he replied as he returned the kiss. He waved goodbye to me.

"Dad, Amelia, I'm leaving," I called towards the closed office door. "See you tomorrow!"

Chapter Eleven:

The Doll Tries to Kill Me

Like any day before a wedding, the next day was incredibly busy. Amelia had the bridesmaids get pedicures, manicures, and massages in the morning. I think it was more relaxing for Amelia than the rest of us. I, on the other hand, was just happy to get a free, relaxing day at the spa.

During the afternoon, the entire wedding party went out for lunch at Mimosa, a seafood joint on the docks. Amelia and Dad gave the wedding party their gifts. I got an 8x10 silver frame engraved with tiny ivy vines along the edges. I was going to put a picture of Eddie and me in it.

I got home about four hours before the rehearsal dinner. I decided to make good use of the time. I put the plaque on the scrapbook and wrapped the wedding gift. After waking up from a

refreshing nap, I went to the closet to get my bridesmaid dress.

The tote cover was thrown open. Not a good sign, because,

after sealing the evil toy in there, I never touched the tote.

Peeking inside I saw the doll box, but no doll. Really bad sign.

After a frantic and fruitless search of the closet, I felt like another

hapless victim in Child's Play. I grabbed the dress and my purse

and sprinted out the door for the Chapel of Love. No possible

danger if Somona and I were far, far away from each other,

right?

I walked into the chapel's library and hung my dress on

the portable clothes rack next to my stepmother-to-be's wedding

dress. For a long time, I stared at the beautiful ball gown-style

dress with the sweetheart neckline. The entire dress was made

out of silk with a Chantilly lace overlay. I hesitated before

touching the long, sheer sleeves for fear of dirtying the ivory

fabric.

My mind began to wander. I find myself in a beautiful

white empire-style wedding dress. Dad is walking me down the aisle where Eddie is waiting for me. The officiate says the magic words and Eddie and I kiss for the first time as husband and wife. I was so lost in my dream world I barely felt the hand on my shoulder.

"Shelly," Amelia said softly, "the rehearsal's about to start."

My dream fizzled out like a warm, summer wind blowing out a sparkler. "Oh, I'm sorry." I turned to Amelia. "I was just thinking about something. You're going to look so beautiful tomorrow."

Amelia smiled radiantly at me. "Why, thank you, Shelly." Then she leaned closer and whispered conspiratorially to me, "And you, my dear, are going to look gorgeous in your dress."

I smiled sheepishly. "You know what? I wish I were the one getting married tomorrow."

"It'll happen, Shelly."

"You really think so?"

"You and Eddie are meant to be together."

I nodded as I set my purse on a nearby table. "Oh, I know, and I really, really want to spend the rest of my life with him. I've never felt this way about anyone."

Amelia grinned at me. "Your time will come, Shelly. Trust me." She and I walked side-by-side out of the room and into the auditorium.

The rehearsal went without a hitch. The ceremony was going to be very typical. Dad and Amelia both love tradition, but they have written their own vows. Throughout the rehearsal, I forced myself not to cry as I tried to get rid of the lump in my throat.

Then came the very tasty rehearsal dinner of the lobster rolls and salad dishes. I felt like the odd man out with all of the couples at the two tables. Dad and Amelia, of course, were there. But there was also Bruce and his girlfriend, Libby Elfstar, Robin and his girlfriend, Brooke Luptin, Lisa and Dirk, and Roger and his supermodel girlfriend, Veronica Elfinson. Even Sabrina Tolkin, Amelia's Welkie hairdresser, was there with her boyfriend. I didn't care because tomorrow was going to be the first wedding where I would be bringing a date. A date who would make the other women drool with envy!

By the time I got home, it was almost ten o'clock, and I was wiped out. I went straight to bed after changing into my rainbow print, drawstring pajamas pants, and matching blue top. I immediately fell into a deep sleep, lulled by the pitter-patter of the sleet falling outside my house.

Unexplained noises woke me from a peaceful sleep. The glaring red digits on my alarm clock read 2:08 in the morning. I lay in bed as my hearing began to filter out the pounding of my heart, the clanging and banging of the heaters, and the light, child-like footsteps echoing across my kitchen floor. My blood suddenly ran cold. Since I was the only person in the house, there were only two possible answers to the mysterious footsteps. Either a super-smart baby had broken in or the doll was alive. I feared it was the latter. I gathered up my courage and slowly opened my bedroom door.

The creepy doll was walking around my kitchen. She jumped up onto one of the chairs twice her height and climbed onto the kitchen table. She sauntered over to my purse. It only took her a few seconds before she pulled out my cell phone.

She flipped it open and began dialing the first number she came to. After this, I was going to keep my cell phone near me at all times.

"Hello?" I could hear Eddie's voice on the other line.

"Wanna play?" the doll spoke for the first time with a disembodied, female voice. It gave me the heebie-jeebies. "Wanna play? Wanna play?" it repeated over and over again in a scary, sing-song voice.

"Shelly, what's going on?" Eddie asked over the phone, apprehension in his voice. He finally realized he wasn't talking to me. "Who is this?" he snapped.

"Eddie!" I shouted, loud enough for the vampire to hear me on the other end of the phone.

The doll whirled around to face me with her super evil smile. Dropping the phone on the floor, the thing vaulted off the table and onto the living room carpet. "Let's play! Let's play!" it chanted in that same even voice as it charged at me with a large cleaver in its little, plastic hand.

I slammed my bedroom door, just in the nick of time, as the doll rammed it with a resounding thud. Locking the door, I quickly collected my shattered nerves. What did I have to protect myself from the doll? A pillow would be ineffective against a knife-wielding toy. A piece of clothing or bedding would have the same result.

As I debated my situation, the doorknob began shaking violently. Dropping to my knees, I peered under the door. Nobody was there. The doll must have jumped to the doorknob and was now trying to unlock the door, or worse, break it down. Crap and double crap.

A car pulled into my driveway, and that's when I decided to get out of the house. Throwing on an old grey hooded sweatshirt over my blue pajama top, I frantically began to look around for my sneakers until I remembered they were in the kitchen. After throwing on my slippers, I heaved open one of the two-bedroom windows. Fortunately, it was only a two-foot drop, but my feet slipped out from under me when I hit the ground. Except for getting all wet, I was unharmed. Carefully, I went to the front of the house. Eddie was already inside the kitchen shouting my name and had a gun drawn. He had turned on the lights. I began pounding on the door to get his attention. "Open up, Eddie!" I shouted.

My boyfriend whirled around at the sound of my voice. He ran and unlocked the door. "Shelly, are you okay?" he asked as he pulled me inside. "God, babe, you're all wet. What's going on?"

"Doll!" was all I could get out. Somona came running at us with knife in hand. An evil laugh escaped her lips as she heaved the knife in our direction. "You should have played with me!" she said.

Eddie stepped in front of me and was about to release a force field spell when the knife pierced his shoulder. He yanked it out. "You were right, Shelly."

"I told you. Now how do we get rid of it?"

"I would torch it, but that blasted knife went right through a muscle in my shoulder." My brain quickly came up with a plan. I grabbed the can opener in the kitchen sink and flung it at the doll who was laughing maniacally. There was a rip of plastic as the opener sliced off Somona's head, and the doll dropped to the ground, lifeless.

"Did you just decapitate a doll with a can opener?" Eddie

asked as he mentally told his shoulder to heal.

"It was the closest weapon I could find." I glanced at the doll, praying that I had successfully killed it. "So, what now?"

"I could torch it."

What is with guys and fire? "I think my landlord might have a problem if we set off the smoke alarm."

"I could torch it at my house." He turned to go. "Let's put the remains in a garbage bag.

"Good idea, Eddie," I said, "but let's double-bag or better yet, triple-bag it."

Eddie noticed my trembling body. "Do you want to stay at my place for the rest of the night?"

I nodded. "After what just happened, I really don't want to be alone." I quickly packed an overnight bag while Eddie scooped the doll and its head into a triple-bagged garbage bag. We left the house a few minutes later.

When we arrived at his house, I was shivering from my cold, wet clothes and the bad scare. I took a long, warm shower and changed into one of Eddie's sweatshirts and a pair of green lounge pants. Instead of going to the guest bedroom, I walked down the oak spiral staircase that led to the living room. Eddie was sitting on his blue pinstripe couch. The oak coffee table was pulled up close to the couch and was strewed with papers and old books. A fire was roaring in the stone fireplace, keeping the entire room warm. "Hi," I said softly as I sat down beside the vampire. I pulled my legs under me and leaned against him.

Eddie looked up from the research he was doing. "Feeling better, babe?" he asked as he gave me a gentle kiss on the lips.

I nodded. "Thanks for letting me stay over."

"Shelly, I should have believed you when you said something was wrong with the doll."

"It's been creeping me out ever since I got it." I began to unleash my worries on Eddie. "And when nobody believed me, I thought for sure I was seeing things."

Eddie pulled me close to him. "It's all right, babe. I believe you now."

"I know you do, honey. So, how are we going to get rid of the Chucky stand-in?"

"Let me take care of it while you get some sleep."

I shook my head. "No way. I won't be able to sleep until I see that doll destroyed."

"I think I've figured out a way to get rid of it."

"Let's hear it."

"We put the doll in a salt circle and torch it."

"You just want to use your fire spell, don't you?"

"Of course."

I sighed. "I kind of want to torch it."

"Well, okay. All we need is an aerosol can and ignition source."

"Awesome, I'll get the salt and the aerosol can. You can be the ignition source."

"I'll get the doll and meet you outside on the driveway."

While I waited for Eddie, I poured a thick circle of salt on the gravel driveway. My vampire soon appeared with a moving trash bag over his shoulder. "Don't tell me it's still alive!"

"It must have put its head back on while in the bag," Eddie answered as he tore open the bags with his bare hands and dumped the doll unceremoniously inside the circle.

"Next time we deal with a demonic doll, we're putting the pieces in separate bags."

"Live and learn, that's us," Eddie said, stepping away from the circle.

Somona had placed her head on backward and was now turning it around correctly. "I want to play with you," she said.

"Let's play 'Burn the Doll," I said, spraying the air freshener can at the creepy toy.

"Nebulae," Eddie said as he let loose a small fireball in the path of the spray.

A dinner plate-size ball of fire melted Somona into a puddle of smoldering plastic. I looked at my handsome boyfriend. "I feel so much better now," I said, "and I feel so empowered. I'll be able to sleep soundly for the rest of the night."

Chapter Twelve:
A Wedding and a Surprise

It took me a few seconds to remember where I was when I woke up the next morning. I had fallen asleep on Eddie's couch. A pillow was now tucked under my head, and a quilt had been draped over my body. I glanced at the wall clock. It read 9:05. Eddie must have gone to bed when the sun rose at six. I got off the couch and shuffled into the kitchen.

A set of keys were sitting on top of a note next to my purse. I opened it up and began to read it aloud. "'Shell, here's the stuff you needed. I went over to check on your house. Jordan's safe in her stable. The keys are to the car waiting outside for you. See you at the wedding. Love, Eddie.'" I looked out the kitchen window facing the road. To my delight, the peanut car was sitting in the gravel driveway. The sun was shining, the doll was gone, and Dad and Amelia were getting married. Yep, this was going to be a great day.

The rest of the day leading up to the wedding was very busy. I showered, ate breakfast, and then went out to get some last-minute items before the big event. When I got to the Chapel at 1:30 that afternoon, Lisa assigned me the job of arranging the wedding programs in little baskets at all three of the doors leading into the auditorium. That took about fifteen or so minutes. Then Lisa told the wedding party to get dressed.

The library was in complete but ordered chaos when I came in. I put on my slip and nylons before getting into my bridesmaid dress. Thank God, it had only one zipper which went all the way up the back. "Lisa," I asked, "could you zip me up?"

"Sure," she said as she came over. "Do you still want me to do your makeup?" Since Lisa wasn't in the wedding party, she was wearing a lovely white dress with a mint green blazer.

I nodded. "Oh, definitely a makeup bag, and Lisa can any girl into a beauty queen. "But after Sabrina does our hair."

"Girls, would you help me with my dress?" Amelia called to us.

Lisa and my mouths dropped when we saw Amelia step out from behind the changing curtain. She looked exquisite in her wedding dress. "Wow!" I said. "Dad's going to be knocked off his feet."

Amelia laughed. "Well, I hope not. He still needs to participate in the ceremony." She turned around after handing us her train.

Libby came into the room. Her short blond hair was held back with a thin headband. "Amelia, look at you. You look lovely. I told you that was the perfect dress."

"Thank you, Libby."

It took all three of us to fasten the train onto the dress. Twenty-five minutes later, we were all done with the zipping and buttoning. It was a good thing because Sabrina, the other bridesmaid came into the room, all ready to go.

Sabrina is a plump Welkie who looks to be in her late fifties, but is almost three hundred years old. Welkies age very slowly. Her salt-and-pepper hair was thrown back into a bun, and we all knew the hairstyle we would be sporting. She pulled a jar of purple, magical hair gel from her blue canvas bag. After carefully rubbing it into my, Amelia's, and Libby's hair, she pulled out a magic wand and said, "Repairo hair!" Within seconds, our hair was perfect, individual hairstyles complete with bobby pins and elastics.

While I was admiring my hair with Lisa's hand-held mirror, my friend turned to me. "All right, Shelly. Let's make you a beautiful bridesmaid!"

It was exactly three o'clock when the organ music began to play which we waited outside the auditorium. I could hear the low murmur of the crowd inside. The doors were opened and the procession began. First, Libby walked down the aisle, then Sabrina, and then I. Cameras flashed over and over again, blinding me as I tried to casually find my boyfriend. I knew that he wouldn't be sitting in a pew by a window, but finding him in this crowd would prove difficult.

Shelly, I'm sitting in the second to last row. I took care of everything. Relax and enjoy your father's wedding.

I casually turned my head and spotted Eddie sitting at the end of the aisle with a camera in his hand. I smiled at him,

praying his pictures would come out all right in this auditorium. I
felt myself relax for the first time since the doll came into my life.

The wedding was so beautiful. Amelia's face was aglow
as she held hands with her husband-to-be. I had never seen
Dad happier as he told Amelia he would love her forever and
ever. Tonight was going to be the first of many nights they would
not have to spend alone. Many of the guests had tears in their
eyes. I shed a few happy tears myself. I was so glad I didn't Lisa
let put mascara on me, or it would be running down my cheeks.

I snuck a glance at my brother who smiling broadly, as he
shared Dad and Amelia's happiness. There were no tears in his
eyes. No way was he going to cry in front of his friends

After the ceremony, the photographer spent about an
hour and a half taking g pictures of the wedding party. I was still
wondering what Eddie had meant by "I took care of everything."
Even when the guests were shaking hands and congratulating
the married couple, Eddie still wouldn't tell me what he did. That
annoyed me just a tad.

After a very delicious catered meal of stuffed chicken breast, scallop potatoes, and a vegetable medley. I glanced over at Eddie's table He was sitting with Dirk, Lisa, Count Stoker, and Countess Stoker. Dirk had been hired by Dad and Amelia to be the DJ at the reception. They all had vegetarian dishes: the pasta primavera and fruit salads. I gave a little wave to Eddie.

Finally, after the toasts, Dad and Amelia did their first dance to "Have I Told You Lately That I Love You?" I watched them wrapped in each other's arms. Thankfully, Dad didn't do any of his weird stretching. Once they finished their dance, Dirk announced for other couples to join them.

"May I have this dance, Shelly?"

I looked over my shoulder to see Eddie standing next to my chair. "I don't know, Eddie," I said hesitantly. "I don't know how to dance."

He grinned at me. "I'm not a great dancer, Shelly, but I'm a pretty good fake dancer."

I pushed back my chair, and Eddie led me to the dance floor. A slow love song that I didn't recognize was playing.

As we danced, I finally asked the question that had been bothering me all day. "So, how did you take care of everything?"

"Earlier today I called the company that makes the dolls," Eddie said as he held one of my hands letting his other hand slip down to the small of my back. "They got in a new shipment, and they are shipping one under your name to the Toy Carnival. It has been gift-wrapped."

"But I thought they had sold out. How did you get one?"

He grinned mischievously. "Well, I hinted how bad it would be if it got out that one of their toys tried to kill a consumer."

"But a spell was put on the doll by a grandmother who was very angry."

"I neglected to mention that little detail."

I looked up at my boyfriend in shock. "Thank you," I stammered, surprised that Eddie went to all the trouble. "Now, when I give the present to Creighton, I guess I'll have to make something up. I'm definitely not telling her about the demon doll." I looked up into Eddie's loving green eyes. "This is why I love you," I whispered in his ear.

"I love you, too, Shelly," Eddie whispered as he kissed my bare shoulder. For the rest of the night, we enjoyed ourselves as we danced and ate some wedding cake. Then it came time for the bouquet toss. All of us single girls gathered behind Amelia as she threw the bunch of flowers high into the air. I don't know how it happened. I wasn't even trying, but somehow I caught it.

Lisa looked at me with a smile. "Shelly, you know what they say. Whoever catches the bouquet is going to be married next."

I had the next day off, and it was a good thing because I was exhausted. At least, my house was demon-doll-free. There were two messages on my cell phone. One was from Dad and Amelia telling me they had made it to Cupid Island, the perfect honeymoon destination, along with their contact information in case of emergency. The next message was from Eddie. "Meet me under the Christmas tree in the town square at seven. Don't be early, and don't be late." This was pretty cryptic, especially from Eddie.

My mother's ring was still missing. Although I was exhausted from all the excitement of the past two days, I did a more intensive search of the house. Nothing showed up. The doll must have destroyed the ring. I sighed heavily. The ring was the only memento that I had of my mother, and now it was gone.

I moped around for the rest of the morning and had a good cry over the loss of the ring. I went to pick up the doll at the Toy Carnival. No grandmotherly witches attacked me with knitting needles. No toys came alive. Nothing happened. Of course, I didn't tell Creighton that I had to replace the doll because the old one was a puddle of melted plastic. I just dropped off the present and apologized for keeping it so long.

The rest of the afternoon, I worked on Eddie's Christmas present. With the help of the photographs, I drew a detailed sketch of my boyfriend leaning against the motorcycle with his right leg on the footrest. Man, he looked fine on paper.

I arrived at the town square right at seven o'clock. The ten-foot-tall evergreen lit up the entire block. I seated myself on a backless marble bench right next to the tree and waited. A cold winter wind swept past me as I wrapped my arms around myself. "Where is he?" I wondered as I checked my watch. It had only been three minutes, but I was getting cold. I was about to call Eddie when I saw him walking towards me. He was wearing his jean jacket over a red sweater and a pair of blue jeans with his casual boots. "What's going on?" I asked. "Where have you—."

He put a finger to my lips to quiet me before getting down on one knee on the snow-covered ground. "Don't talk. Shelly, I can't begin to tell you how much I love you. You're the first person who has made my life complete. I want to spend the rest of my life with you." He paused as he reached into the side pocket of his jacket and pulled out a black, velvet ring box. "Michelle Anderson, will you marry me and become Mrs. Edgar Van Helsing?" he said as he slowly opened up the box.

My jaw dropped in astonishment as I looked from my vampire to the ring glittering inside the box. I recognized the now freshly polished golden band, but there was no old gemstone. In its place was a sparkling, perfectly cut blue diamond. "Yes!" I said, my voice cracking with emotion. "Yes, I will marry you!" Once he was on his feet, I threw my arms around his neck, and we kissed deeply.

"I don't mind the kissing, babe," Eddie said as he gently pulled away from me, "but I want to see how your mom's ring looks on you." He took off my gloves and slipped the ring on my finger.

"Wow!" I said softly as I stared at the ring. It was so beautiful. "It fits perfectly."

"The cool thing is that when we pick out our wedding bands, we can get one that matches."

"Eddie," I said as I continued to stare at the ring, "it's just perfect. I love it." I looked up at him. "How did you pull this off without me knowing?"

He grinned triumphantly. "Well, it wasn't easy. I had Robin steal the ring for me when he picked up you the night we helped decorate the diner."

"And you knew where the ring was all the time."

"Would you have liked it if I had told you what I was doing?"

I couldn't stop smiling at him. "Well, no." Something was still bugging me. Eddie didn't have five hundred or so druci hanging around. So, how could he have paid for the diamond?

Then I remembered what I had discovered in his garage. I was astonished and deeply touched. "You sold the picklemobile to pay for the diamond? But you loved that car."

"Not as much as I love you, Shelly" Then he looked at me suspiciously. "How did you know I sold the car? I certainly wasn't thinking about it just now." Then it dawned on him. "So, you're the one who broke into my garage."

I grinned sheepishly. "It's for part of your Christmas present."

He gave me a forgiving kiss. "Well, I can't wait to see it."

"You'll like it," I assured him. "I have to call my dad and my stepmom." I fished my cell phone out of my purse and dialed Dad's cell. It rang a few times before he answered. "Dad, it's Shelly! Put me on speakerphone so that Amelia can hear the good news, too." I felt Eddie's arms wrap around me to keep me warm. "Dad, Amelia," I said, barely able to contain the excitement in my voice, "Eddie and I are getting married!"

COMING SOON
Reunion of the Undead
My Life Among the Undead: Book 6

Shelly Anderson and her vampire fiancé, Eddie Van Helsing, have faced zombies, possessed dolls, demon spiders, mobsters, and evil sorcerers. But this time Shelly has to overcome her biggest challenge yet: meeting Eddie's family. They put "fun" in dysfunctional. Meet the playboy, the ditzy supermodel, the bigoted ranch owners, and the coffin collector uncle.

The real trouble starts when Eddie is falsely accused of murdering his uncle. Proving her fiancé's innocence is harder than Shelly realizes, especially when everyone hated Uncle Ludwig. Bring out the aspirin and watch out for the nuts falling off the family tree.

ABOUT THE AUTHOR

Camara Bragdon has her master's degree in library and information science and lives in Maine. This is the fifth book in her vampire series, *My Life Among the Undead*. Visit her website at www.camarambragdonauthor.com